BUSHWHACKED—

Russ saw there was no outriding their pursuers.

"Watch yourself, Colcord," he muttered to his companion. "This won't be pleasant, but whatever you do, keep your hand away from that gun."

The approaching quartet spread out as they neared, closing in stony-faced. Russ reined close to Colcord, facing the roughs with cool defiance. "All right, Deuce. What's this all about?"

"Just hand us over the old man," Deuce returned cynically. "We don't want nothing of you."

Colcord trembled with rage and defiance. "If you want money, I ain't got any."

Deuce laughed rancorously. "That I'll believe—after we get done with you." He motioned brusquely to his men.

"All right, boys. Pull 'em down!"

RATTLESNAKE RANGE
was originally published by Jefferson House, Inc.

Rattlesnake Range

by Peter Field

A POWDER VALLEY WESTERN

PUBLISHED BY POCKET BOOKS NEW YORK

RATTLESNAKE RANGE

Jefferson House edition published 1961

POCKET BOOK edition published November, 1974

L

This POCKET BOOK edition includes every word contained
in the original, higher-priced edition. It is printed from
brand-new plates made from completely reset, clear, easy-to-
read type. POCKET BOOK editions are published by POCKET
BOOKS, a division of Simon & Schuster, Inc., 630 Fifth
Avenue, New York, N.Y. 10020. Trademarks registered
in the United States and other countries.

Standard Book Number: 671-75832-2.
Library of Congress Catalog Card Number: 60-10777.
This POCKET BOOK edition is published by arrangement
with William Morrow and Company, Inc. Copyright, ©,
1961, by Jefferson House, Inc. All rights reserved. This
book, or portions thereof, may not be reproduced by any
means without permission of the original publisher: Jefferson House, Inc., 105 Madison Avenue, New York, N.Y. 10016.
Front cover illustration by John Duillo.

Printed in the U.S.A.

Rattlesnake
Range

[1]

"Hey, Stevens! Swat this gnat for me, will yuh?"

It was tall, gangling Ezra who spoke, uncommonly good-humoredly for him, if with an edge of irritation. Sam Sloan, his squat, chunky partner in the little Bar ES horse ranch, promptly jeered scornfully.

"Nuts to your gnats," he rapped tartly. "Just because yuh got a dollar in your jeans don't try to lord it over me, Skinny. I earned it for yuh!"

"You earned it . . . !" Sitting in his saddle straight and dignified, a black patch over one eye that had been lost years ago in a knife fight, Ezra glared from under the black flatbrim hat with his good eye, speechless for once with bristling indignation.

Young and lithe, in the hard prime of vigorous life, Pat Stevens did not so much as check his horse as he glanced obliquely at the huffy pair.

The little mountain town of Ganado was several hours behind them. Now that their prime roan herd had been safely delivered during the early hours of the morning, and their money collected, Ezra and Sam were feeling their oats. It was like them to break into a rousing argument on the way home to Powder Valley. This was one of the ways in which they expressed a keen and enduring respect for each other, since either would have died rather than to show it in any other way.

"I can help you drive stock. I can't help you divide the few dollars, the stuff is worth," replied Pat lazily, hoping to rivet their attention.

Ezra was so incensed by his partner's gall as to miss completely this slur at the quality of their excellent roan strain. "Did yuh hear that?" he cried. *"He* earned a dollar for me, Stevens! I never ran into such barefaced brass in my livelong life!"

7

"Take another look," Sam invited pugnaciously. "I ain't hardly begun to tell you off, Lazy bones."

"Stevens—look here—" began Ezra thickly, choking with anger.

But at the moment the younger man was not paying him any attention. His sharp glance was caught, fixed on some object across the grassy hollow they were passing. Even Sam noted his abstraction, pausing to peer that way. "What yuh lookin' at, boy?" he demanded, forgetting his argument with Ezra completely.

Pat only held up a hand, turning his mount down into the hollow and skirting the buckbrush clumped in its center. The partners followed, struck momentarily silent. They caught up with him a moment later as he sat motionless, staring down at the carcass of a dead steer.

It had been shot, a drying rill of blood marking the bullet hole in the frontal bone of the flat skull. A shoulder and some of the prime ribs had been carved out; yet the animal had not been skinned, an irregular burn on the brown-haired flank plainly revealing its brand.

"Beef thieves!" exclaimed Sloan, easing his bulky weight inside the skin-tight bib overalls he habitually wore. "What brand would yuh take that for, Stevens?"

"Looks like a rough deerhorn. . . . Why, it's Antler, o' course," Ezra caught him up gruffly.

Pat nodded thoughtfully. "It's Ben Cobb's Antler stuff," he assented tersely. "But this isn't Antler range through here. It's waste country—" He glanced about. What he said was true. Except for an occasional patch of grass such as this hollow, the rolling land was a desert of mesquite brush, stunted and dry and useless.

Sam pointed north. "That's right. Cobb's spread lies north along the Culebras. There's better graze up that way. The beef stealers must've choused old Ben's cows down here to avoid being spotted at their dirty work."

"There's more of 'em." Riding back up to the rim of the hollow, Ezra pointed in several directions with a bony forefinger. "I can count six or eight grazin' cows—"

"Let's look around a little." Suiting action to the words, Stevens began to quarter back and forth through the surrounding brush. Within ten minutes he located another beefed steer, its haunch carved out. The plain marks of a pony showed how the meat had been packed out.

Sam rasped the bristly blue stubble covering his chubby jowls while he thought it over. His expression was sober. "Better shove on to Dutch Springs, hadn't we, and report this to the law?" he queried tentatively.

Ezra snorted. A single glance at Stevens' face had told him the answer. "Run along and report if yuh want," he growled scornfully. "Me and Stevens can gather up Cobb's cows and shove 'em along home before more go under."

Taking the hint, Sloan said no more. Without delay the trio combed a score of Antler steers out of the brush and spent time looking for more. Ben Cobb was not a big rancher, and he could ill afford the loss of even a few head.

When a third steer was discovered ruthlessly cut down and butchered, Ezra gave a snarl of suppressed fury. "This could spell grief for every man in Powder Valley if it gets a good start," he burst out.

Pat nodded. "The least we can do is to warn Cobb to watch his stuff more closely," he added briefly. "If these beef thieves are spotted there's a chance they can be washed up in short order."

Throwing the Antler stock together, they headed it home. Although they kept a close watch on the open range there was nothing to attract their notice. It was Pat's guess that the stock killers had got in their work sometime the previous evening; and if so, they were long gone by now.

The rugged foothills of the Culebras rose on their left, climbing a few miles beyond to the heights marked by lofty peaks. Cobb's Antler spread was situated on a wooded bench, and behind it opened grassy canyons which constituted the greater part of old Ben's protected range.

It was crowding midday when Sam gave a cry. "There's Ben's place." He pointed. "Looks like old Cobb was watchin' us—"

They could just make out a tiny figure on the edge of the bench. But when they drew closer this figure had disappeared. Either they had been mistaken or the elderly rancher had hurried to get up a bronc. Yet after the lapse of long minutes he did not reappear. They were beginning to ask themselves what this meant when an unexpected development occurred.

"Hey—!" Letting out an involuntary screech of surprise, Sam hauled his pony up short and glanced sharply about. "Somebody slung a slug at us, Stevens!"

Pat thought he had detected the sound of a bullet as it snipped the brush in its passage. A second later he was sure. "Watch yourselves, you two," he sang out. "We're being fired on, for a fact!"

"I can tell yuh where from." Ez was gruff. He pointed toward the distant Cobb cabin, above them on its bench. "Smoke driftin' across the front of them logs. Look real close and you'll spot it."

Despite the handicap of his missing eye he was right. Stevens tipped his Stetson forward, scratching his head. But it was Sam who let out an explosive protest.

"Yuh mean Ben Cobb is plunkin' at us—?" He swore heartily. "Why, dang the old reprobate! After what we done for him, I'm quittin' right here!" He started to turn his horse away, but delayed, noting despite his outrage that the others did not immediately follow.

Fresh fire from the bench shortly decided them. Pat ducked as a slug whined close overhead, and turned his horse toward the protection of a nearby ledge. "It *is* getting rather warm," he observed unhurriedly.

Ezra still hesitated stubbornly. "We leavin' this stock here?" he demanded.

"Whatever his object is, old Ben can't miss seeing them." Pat's grin flashed coolly. "Of course if you insist on shoving ahead yourself—"

Ez gave up disgustedly, turning back. "The old fool don't know who we are," he insisted, halting the instant he reached safe cover. "We still ought t' warn him of what's goin' on, Stevens!"

Pat agreed without noticeable enthusiasm. "He'll be kind of hard to reach right now," he suggested.

"Hang it—we can circle around!"

Pat's tone was unusually mild. "I still think Cobb's in no mood to be argued with." He glanced from one to the other shrewdly. "My guess is that we can't tell him much he don't already know."

"So are we droppin' it here?" Sam looked hopeful.

Pat delayed briefly before shaking his head. "I didn't say that."

Sloan showed his exasperation. "All right, Smarty. Give it to us in three-letter words."

"It's not only old Ben that's involved here," Stevens pointed out temperately. "His oldest son—Marty—kind of thinks Antler's his—or will be someday. We could hunt up Marty," he added easily, "and tell him about this."

"Marty's sensible, I'll hand him that," seconded Sam suspiciously. "But where is he right now?"

Pat thought that in view of the tense situation into which they had stumbled unawares, young Cobb would almost certainly be found on guard somewhere about the Antler range.

Ezra shrugged. "That's a large order," he grumbled.

Stevens glanced at him levelly. "You're a tracker," he retorted. "Maybe you can scare him up."

Ez made no immediate reply, but his expression was thoughtful. "If it was me," he opined finally, "I'd be scoutin' around through them canyons—"

Pat nodded readily. "We'll try that. It hadn't ought to be too much of a chore to work around into Trap Canyon."

Abandoning their watch on the Antler steers, they pulled away from the protecting ledge. Another shot or two was promptly fired, but they were soon beyond range of the distant marksman. Anyone watching their course might have said they were bent on leaving the locality; but once well beyond sight of the Cobb ranch they circled back. Less than an hour later they were climbing the foothills and dropping down a long rough slant into Trap Canyon.

Ben Cobb claimed several canyons as a part of his scattered range, but Trap was the largest and certainly the best. It was also broken, irregular, and confusing to anyone who did not know the ground well. Sam glanced about him with scant interest.

"Be real lucky if we don't get lost in here," he commented disparagingly. "How come yuh figure to find anything here is beyond me."

His companions did not bother to reply. Despite Sloan's remarks, however, he was not far behind them in diligence as they proceeded to search the various arms of the canyon. Moving warily at first, they found little cause for caution, having struck Trap Canyon a couple of miles above the Cobb ranch. Scattered Antler stock was to be seen grazing here and there. But evidently no very close guard over them was considered necessary.

"Looks like yuh draw a blank, Stevens," Ezra expressed himself deliberately at last.

Without reply Pat made for a rocky shoulder, beyond which a reach of the canyon opened out into tumbled range stretching away to the north. Passing the obstruction, he drew rein to gaze that way for so long that Sam could not help noticing it.

"See anything?" he called.

Without responding, Stevens waved them forward. They lost no time in joining him. Neither needed to be shown what had attracted his attention.

Half a mile away over the rolling brush a rider was coming toward them. He moved slowly, and it was soon apparent that he was leading another bronc which bore on its back an undistinguishable burden.

"We found him, eh?" For long minutes they sat watching and waiting. It was Sam who finally spoke again. "Why, that ain't Marty Cobb, Stevens! It's—it looks like—"

"It's young Russ Cobb instead of Marty," Pat interposed, pushing his horse forward as he spoke. "And I don't like the looks of that load he's packing."

They thrust on toward the approaching rider, and it was presently plain that Russ Cobb saw them. He halted, and Ezra thought he was about to draw his rifle from the saddle boot. Pat got it too. He waved reassuringly.

"Take it easy, Cobb," he called from between cupped hands. "It's Pat Stevens, boy. Don't you know me?"

After a moment Russ appeared to relax. He came on, watching keenly until he had assured himself of their identity. Stevens saw now that it was a man who was hanging limply over the led horse and carefully lashed on. It made him increase his pace, his face creased into lines of sobriety.

"Who is that, Russ?" he called as he neared. "It can't be your brother Mart—! What happened?"

Young Russ Cobb drew rein a few yards away to stare at them glumly, his face a mask of stoic tragedy. "It's Marty all right," he brought out tightly. "He's been shot, Stevens! I don't know whether he'll live or not—"

"But he's not gone yet?" Pat slid hurriedly out of the saddle and strode forward. "Lend a hand here, Ez. We'll have a look."

"I—did all I could." But young Cobb did not object to their doing what they could. He watched dazedly as Ezra and Pat unloosened the ropes and lowered his brother Marty to the ground.

Marty Cobb was somewhere in the neighborhood of thirty, nearly a dozen years older than Russ. A tall, raw-boned man, hardened by unremitting labor, he was the virtual head of Antler—or had been until today. A curly stubble fringing his rocky face showed how hard he had driven himself of late.

He had been shot through the left shoulder, danger-ously close to the lung, and was unconscious and mut-tering deliriously. Pat noted with approval that Russ had bound his wound with dry moss under a clean kerchief. If the bleeding had not been altogether stopped, little more could be done at the moment.

"You tied him up, I see. That's fine, Russ." Pat spoke without haste. "All you can do now is to get him home and go for a doctor." Squatting on his heels, he turned to glance upward inquiringly. "How did this happen, any-way?"

"Pack Traver shot him," supplied the young fellow savagely. "I didn't see it happen, but I heard the shot. And five minutes later I seen Traver runnin'."

"Couldn't be any mistake, eh?" Pat was following Cobb's talk closely.

"About that paint horse of Pack's, yuh mean?" Russ shook his head vehemently. "Not in a million years, Stevens! It was him, not a shadow of doubt about it!"

If Sam and Ezra exchanged significant glances, they said nothing. No one could have missed the meaning of Russ Cobb's words. Pack Traver was the owner of the little T Square, which adjoined the Antler. There was al-ways friction between the smaller spreads on this range. None could hope to branch out without more grass. This was the first time in a long while that such antagonism had flared into open warfare.

Moreover, the situation went far to explain old Ben Cobb's belligerence at a time when they were trying to do him a favor.

Pat shook his head minutely, not bothering to discuss details. "I'm sorry to hear it," he said after a pause. "You better get Marty straight home, boy. Whatever you do after that," he pursued reasonably, "try to take it slow. Will you do that?"

Cobb's grief-stricken face knotted with a flash of fury. "I'll do whatever's called for," he jerked out harshly. "Thanks for nothing, Stevens! The Cobbs won't be run off of Antler if I know it!"

Pat prudently omitted a response, helping Ezra to lift the wounded man back on the led horse. When he spoke at last, his voice was surprisingly moderate.

"Never mind. I sure hope Marty pulls through this. If he does, he'll have something to say on his own account."

Russ snorted, saying no more. They watched him push on, grim and undaunted, his tough young face fixed like iron. Not till he drew beyond earshot did Pat voice his final comment.

"Too bad. I don't think much of his convicting evidence," he said mildly. "He could be all wrong about Pack Traver. But that won't matter to him—or to old Ben either." He shook his head. "I'm afraid this spells real trouble between those ranches, with no way to head it off. I know I'm done trying, before I get in over my head. Let's go home."

[2]

The early sun was slanting along Dutch Springs' single business street as Pat Stevens jogged into the little cow town on the second day following his adventure with the Bar ES partners. Few people were about at this hour; a swamper or two was opening and mopping out stores. But Stevens was in time to observe Jess Lawlor, the Powder County sheriff, fussing over a cow pony in front of his tiny adobe office.

Riding down there out of curiosity, Stevens lifted a hand in greeting and sat watching the lawman for a moment. Obviously Lawlor was preparing for a trip.

"What's up, Jess?"

Lawlor shrugged. "Little difficulty over in Ganado," he said with morning gruffness. "Probably won't amount to much. But I got to go and see."

Digesting this scanty information, Pat thought swiftly. He had a strong suspicion that he knew what the trouble over there might be, but he was not naive enough to ask for details. "That's odd," he commented cheerfully. "Lucky for me, too. It happens I've got business over that way—if you don't object to my riding along?"

Jess looked faintly surprised. "Why should I, Stevens?"

"No reason, of course," Pat agreed innocently. "I just don't want you to think I was inviting myself." Since that was exactly what he was doing, he thought himself fortunate when the sheriff neglected to make any further comment.

Jess was ready presently, and they shoved off. It was a brisk, keen morning in early summer, with a promise of later heat. The horses set an energetic pace. For several miles the Ganado road followed the Bar ES trail, and for reasons of his own Pat hoped that neither of the partners would put in an appearance today.

For once he was in luck. They passed the Bar ES turnoff without event, pushing steadily on toward Ganado. Once the sun had warmed his broad shoulders, Lawlor was voluble enough in his brusque way. But if Pat waited for the lawman to make any further reference to his errand this morning he waited in vain. Jess was the taciturn sort, not overly imaginative. He took his duties as a usual thing with great calm. Pat had had experience of Lawlor's bullheaded stubbornness in the past, and he contented himself now with whatever developments might come.

Toward midmorning they began to draw near to Ganado. Similar in size to Dutch Springs, the sawmill and supply town was situated in the mouth of a canyon on the edge of the lofty Culebras, its narrow street crowded in between the tight rows of boardinghouses, bars and business establishments.

Ganado was always a busy place. They passed a freight rig or two rumbling by, and saw men riding into town along the branching ranch trails. Pat presently took particular notice of one man who came racking along from behind and showed signs of soon overtaking them. Lawlor finally noticed his fixed attention.

"Who is that?" he growled, turning for his own look.

Pat was in no hurry to reply. "It's Pack Traver," he said finally. "What business would T Square have in town today, I wonder?" As he spoke he was thinking about those slain steers, the beef of which could only have been sold in Ganado.

Jess only grunted. "Whatever it is, Traver's comin' at full steam."

The rancher drew up on them a moment later. A

blocky, red-faced man who made up with bluff what he lacked in brains, Pack narrowed his flinty eyes as he recognized Sheriff Lawlor.

"Howdy, Jess." He spoke boldly, obviously waiting to learn whether the other man was interested in his movements, not taking his sly glance off Lawlor. Pat was no less interested in what this casual meeting might bring, having no way of knowing whether Ben Cobb had reported his difficulties with Traver or not. But apparently Jess had nothing to say at the moment.

"Traver." Nodding curtly, he looked austerely away.

For his part, Pat had no intention of letting the matter drop. "What is this I hear about a little hassle with your neighbors, Pack?" he asked.

Traver shot him a dark look. "No trouble," he denied with suspicious promptness. "What are you drivin' at, Stevens?"

"It got to me that old Ben Cobb was on the war path," Pat insisted coolly. "He lost some steers—and I understand Marty got winged the other day."

"So? And how does that concern me?"

"I heard he's blaming it all on you," Pat replied flatly. "Understand, I don't pretend to say whether this is true or not, Traver. But personally, I'd consider it smart for you to stay home for a day or two."

Pack put on an air of disgust. "There yuh go! Carryin' tales like a lot of other hombres on this range. . . . Let me get this straight," he rasped. "Are yuh tryin' to queer me with the law with this phony story, Stevens—or what are yuh after?"

"Not at all." Pat visibly cooled, aware once more of his active dislike of the man. "Lawlor probably knows as much as I do—which I'll admit isn't much. I'm beginning to wonder why I even bother to give you good advice!"

"Well, then, save it," Traver snarled arrogantly. "When a man disputes my right to use the public road, I usually want to know why. And his reason better be good!"

Pat promptly reined over to the side of the trail. "My

mistake, mister. Don't delay yourself longer on my account."

Pack spared a bare second to asssure himself that Jess Lawlor did not intend to step into the situation. He rammed a spur into his nervous bronc then and shot past them, savagely curbing the spooked horse with his rein and cantering briskly on toward Ganado. Jess gazed after him speculatively, his mouth set in firm lines.

"If I had any hankerin' to be a horse," he remarked presently, "I sure wouldn't insist on bein' in his string."

Pat's grunt was humorless. "Don't know why, but I never did trust a man who's hard on animals," he returned with equal brevity. "Traver is."

Pack Traver had disappeared when they rode into Ganado a short time later. Not improbably he was ensconced in some saloon. Pat put him out of his mind, although he did not forget the other, and looked the town over.

Ganado still had some of the aspects of a frontier town. Few of its crowding frame structures were painted; here and there a crumbling log cabin still clung high up on the narrow canyon walls. The street was humming with activity. From here a stage line ran up into the mountains, and mining rigs busily loaded supplies for the interior. Cowboys, miners and sawmill hands, blanketed Utes, gawking travelers and dapper drummers crowded the boardwalks.

Reining in at a rack before the Miners Rest Hotel, Sheriff Lawlor made the gruff excuse of business and moved off. Pat was content to wait, dismounting to stretch and move about while he gauged the temper of this place. No one paid him any attention as they jostled past on the busy plank sidewalk. Eyeing the busy strollers, he noted a sprinkling of gamblers, range men on the loose, and the usual town loafers.

Like Dutch Springs this was also Jess Lawlor's territory; a tough deputy was posted in Ganado to keep an eye on things. Pat was wondering if any echo of the range strife had filtered into town when he saw a man he knew slightly standing in the doorway of a gambling hall.

It was Chuck Stober, owner of the huge War Ax spread, which dominated this end of Powder Valley and lapped over into the Culebra foothills. Stevens had heard that Stober had been prospering of late, until War Ax had become little short of a mountain empire. The man looked the part, his hat perched at a cocky angle, a stogie clamped in his pugnacious jaw.

"Stober'll know," Pat thought, starting to shove through the crowding pedestrians in the other's direction. "I'll ask him about Traver and Cobb. Maybe he can straighten them out, for that matter."

He did not get far. Before he had reached the middle of the street a yell rang out. On the instant men began to melt away, many running, as if sharply aware of what was coming. Turning on his heel, Stevens saw Pack Traver standing spread-legged in the open, a mask of cold anger stamped on his blunt red features.

Alone in a suddenly opened space, Pack's attention was fixed malevolently on another man. Backing slowly out of the way, Pat was not at all surprised to find that it was young Russ Cobb.

"What's the big idea of trailin' me around, kid?" Traver ripped truculently.

Halting uncertainly, Cobb looked briefly daunted. But he did not avoid the direct challenge. "Right now I'm looking for the sawbones, Pack. Marty's been bad—as you ought to know!" he blurted indignantly.

"Don't lie!" Traver was working himself into a cold fury. "Yuh been followin' me—and what's more, yuh were spreadin' crazy stories!"

Russ looked astonished, his own resentment flaring. "Me?" he barked. "What could I say about you that ain't true? The whole range must be onto your rotten game by now, Traver!"

Traver's face went black. "Never mind! I ain't arguin' with yuh! Get down on your hands and knees," he ordered harshly. "Crawl up to me and apologize, and maybe I'll let yuh off light this time!"

Listening, Pat Stevens was frankly astonished by the

overbearing arrogance of the older man. Obviously he was bent on crushing young Cobb's pride, molding him to his brazen will for good and all. Or worse still, Pack meant to crowd the boy beyond endurance and, using his rage as an excuse, to kill him.

Pat glanced quickly about, asking himself where Sheriff Lawlor could be at the moment. Not even Lawlor's deputy was in evidence. Nor did Chuck Stober, the War Ax owner, show any intention of taking part in the affair, standing calmly in the doorway opposite and watching.

Russ Cobb was not so immature as to be altogether rattled by this treacherous bully's onslaught. He waved a hand contemptuously.

"I've got no time for you now," he declared doggedly. "Maybe later, Traver. Since you're begging for a settlement!"

He started to turn away. Pack may have taken it for a retreat. Determined to seize his advantage, he ripped out an oath. "Hold on, there——" With the exclamation, he jerked at his gun.

The result was wholly unexpected. Young Russ whirled back, his Colt flashing out on the instant. Two shots crashed almost together. But it was plain to Pat Stevens that, although taken at a disadvantage, Cobb had strangely enough been a shade the quicker. He was also the most accurate. At the moment that his hat flew off, Pack Traver threw up his arms, staggered, and then crashed backwards to lie motionless.

"What's the meanin' of this?" a harsh voice exploded in the suddenly thick silence. Sheriff Lawlor came striding forward authoritatively. He wrested young Cobb's six-gun from his now numb hand and took charge of him on the spot. "Drag your killin' right into town, will yuh?" he rapped sourly at Russ.

With the lawman's arrival other men crowded into the open space, closing in about Traver's prone form and staring morbidly. Lawlor glowered at them briefly.

"Come on, you," he snapped, tightening his grip on Cobb. "I'm takin' you down to the jail, boy."

Evidently the sheriff had not seen enough of the action to understand it completely. Pat took the time to note that Chuck Stober was still watching imperturbably without movement. He thought it time to intercede, and was about to push through to Lawlor's side when a hitch occurred.

"Mr. Lawlor!"

A clear feminine voice rang firmly through the hubbub of muttering men. All turned to glance around. Pat recognized the slim, graceful girl who made her way forward coolly. Even those who did not paid the tribute of deference to her luxuriant copper-hued hair and blazing, level blue eyes. She was Penny Colcord, daughter of the stalwart Saw Buck owner, a grizzled pioneer respected by every man in the mountain territory.

"What is it now, ma'am?" Jess Lawlor managed to look disgruntled, but he waited for her to speak.

Penny Colcord thrust close, giving these men the full benefit of her imposing self-possession. She faced the lawman squarely. "You may not have seen exactly what happened here, Sheriff," she said composedly. "Surely you're not arresting Russ Cobb simply for protecting himself?"

"Sure of that, are yuh?" He eyed her stonily.

"Nonsense. Of course I am. Anyone here will tell you that Pack Traver forced Russ to act. Traver drew first, if that will ease your conscience!"

"That's one story. I intend to hear all sides of this, Miss—"

"I saw it too, Jess," Pat put in mildly. "Let her tell it —and I'll put a finger on anything she gets wrong."

Unwilling to prolong this talk, Lawlor knew when he was stumped. "Well . . . give it to me," he grumbled.

The girl related a clear, precise account of what had happened. Stevens nodded agreement at the end. "No flaws in that," he acknowledged. "Pack Traver was honing for what he got—and Cobb certainly had no choice, unless *he* wanted to be lying here." He glanced around at the listening men. "Any corrections?"

None were offered. Out of the corner of his eye Pat

observed that Chuck Stober, the War Ax baron, had moved away at last. But Jess Lawlor professed not to be wholly satisfied. "I don't know." His tone was stubborn. "I'll say now that I was called over here on Traver's claim that he was being crowded into a corner by these Cobbs."

Penny Colcord's exclamation did not have a pleasant sound. "You can't mean that you were brought to Ganado to witness that conscienceless scamp performing some of his ruthless work?" she demanded hotly.

Lawlor looked uncomfortable as a chuckle or two was heard. "Don't be puttin' words in my mouth," he retorted. "Pack reported trouble with his neighbors. He may have seen this comin', ma'am! After what happened, even a fool could tell he wasn't wrong."

"Mr. Lawlor," Penny caught him up severely. "You seem to have listened to Pack Traver's story. Did you ask any one else at all?" She paused scornfully. "Will you listen to me now?"

Much annoyed, Jess avoided her blazing level glance. Plainly her clear-skinned charm threw him off balance, as it did others present. But he was determined to be literally fair. "I asked once for the whole thing!" he snorted.

Penny nodded. "Are you aware that beef thieves have been busy on Ben Cobb's range for the past three weeks —and that Pack Traver was seen more than once?" she asked pointedly.

Lawlor was startled. "I knew old Ben lost a head or two—"

"He lost two dozen or more," she cut him off tartly. "I need not ask whether you rode out to investigate! . . . And do you know," she drove on hardily, "that Marty Cobb was treacherously shot two days ago—that he may not live—and that Traver was seen riding away from the spot?"

Lawlor scratched his head, staring at young Russ oddly. "Is this all true, boy?" he queried.

Russ shrugged. "I could have told you so if you'd

asked! And so could Dad. But we didn't see you out there."

"I'll have to make a call on old Ben." The sheriff turned to a reputable merchant in the crowd. "Did you see this deal here in the street, Smathers?"

The store proprietor indicated briefly that he had. Jess grunted. "All right. Give me your slant," he directed curtly.

Smathers gave an account identical at every point with the girl's, and adhering meticulously to the facts. Lawlor nodded conclusively at the end.

"That's three stories that jibe." He turned to Russ, handing back the latter's gun. "Under the circumstances I'm not justified in holdin' yuh, boy," he acknowledged simply.

"I should think not!" Penny Colcord looked at Russ, obviously hoping for approval of her stout support. But young Cobb appeared not to notice.

"Thanks for nothing!" He gave the faintly chagrined lawman a glance of freezing disgust. "Next time take the trouble to inquire into the facts before you make an arrest, will you, Lawlor?"

Then, to the surprise of them all, he brushed through the circle and strode off.

[3]

Nothing further occurred at Ganado in connection with the range feud. Stevens stayed in town only long enough to assure himself that Russ Cobb had left without being molested further. Then he rode home alone.

He spent Thursday and Friday of that week at work on his comfortable Lazy Mare ranch. On Saturday he rode over to the Bar ES for a day with the crusty partners. No more news had come through regarding the Ganado range trouble. But early the following week Pat realized that he had not yet been able to put the Cobbs wholly out of his mind.

For two more days he resisted the strong impulse to inquire further into the matter on his own account. On Wednesday, abruptly capitulating, he set off early in the morning, striking off southward across the range.

The sun was only an hour or so high when he drew near Ben Cobb's little Antler once more. Approaching by the ranch trail, he was within a hundred yards before, rounding a rocky outcrop edging the bench, his eyes fell on the somnolent log ranch shack. It was a momentary disappointment not to see young Russ at least working about the pole corrals. But, as it happened, there was not a sign of life to be detected anywhere about the place.

Riding up calmly, Pat drew rein and glanced about. "Anybody home?" he called.

There was no response. The slab door did not stir, nor could he detect any sounds of movement from within. He was about to turn for a look around when, with a jar, he suddenly realized that someone was watching him intently from the far corner of the cabin.

Swinging that way, he found old Ben himself glowering at him. "What yuh after?" the old fellow growled, showing no sign of recognition.

"Howdy, Cobb. I just dropped by to see how you were doing." Ignoring the battered rifle the other still warily clutched, he watched the rancher's wrinkled face carefully. Dark and weather-beaten, Cobb might have been taken for an Indian.

He shook his grizzled head stubbornly. "No yuh didn't," he contradicted flatly. "Yuh was hopin' I'd be gone, wasn't yuh? Every hombre that shows up here is after somethin' or other, Stevens. So haul your freight."

Pat's laugh was easy. "After the troubles I hear you've been having, I can't blame you for being suspicious," he conceded. "If I wanted anything at all from you, old-timer, it would only be an apology—"

Ben wouldn't bite. "You won't get one," he declared. "You or anyone else!"

Pat waved this aside, relating how he and the Bar ES owners had run across several beefed Antler steers on the waste range several miles to the south. "We gathered up a bunch of your strays and drove them home for you that day," he concluded. "And all we got for it was some hot slugs!" He grinned as he finished to show there were no hard feelings.

Old Cobb watched him steadily throughout. "You, was it?" The fact didn't seem to interest him much. "Wouldn't have took no chances if I had known who it was!"

Pat showed faint surprise, his tone sobering. "Man, we were trying to do you a favor! Don't you get that?"

"Yuh say so," Cobb retorted hardily.

"We wouldn't let it go like that. We tried to hunt up Marty that day—"

"And found him—with a bullet?"

"We found Russ packing him home," Stevens corrected sharply. "The boy must have told you, Cobb. Why do you persist in this foolish attitude?"

Old Ben made a violent gesture. "Told yuh to drag out of here, didn't I?" he rasped forbiddingly. "I don't need your help, Stevens. And I don't want it!"

Pat looked at him for a long moment, then shrugged. "I guess you mean it at that," he decided dryly. He gathered up his reins, ready to turn away. "Just try to remember that I mean well by you. If you change your mind, let me know."

"I will if I do." Clamping his lips shut sternly, Ben did not leave the impression that he was likely to experience a change of heart within the immediate future.

Pat turned his horse and started off. As he jogged down off the bench without a backward look, he thoughtfully turned the situation over. Despite the crusty rancher's antagonism Stevens was not yet ready to wash his hands of the business.

"I never even got a chance to ask how Marty's doing," he mused ruefully, accusing himself now of not being sufficiently patient with the crotchety old man. "Or to ask if Russ was staying close to the ranch these days.

He could be in line for trouble, whether he knows it or not. Pack Traver must have some friends."

Thinking of Traver turned his thoughts toward the T Square. Unmarried and somewhat misanthropic by nature, Pack had employed one elderly puncher, old Kip McKinley. Wondering whether McKinley was still living there alone, with Traver gone, Stevens turned that way. T Square range was a ride of only a couple of miles across the broken range from Antler, and he was soon on it. Traver's run-down ranch was not much farther.

"With Pack out of the way there might be evidence of his beefing steers," he reflected. "I wonder if old Ben or Russ thought to look?"

The bare possibility made him approach circumspectly; and it was just as well that he did so. As he paused to scan the outspread T Square buildings from the cover of scrub oak atop a rise, he was surprised to note signs of considerable activity about the place.

Horses stood in the yard, and several men appeared to be busy about the corrals. After watching for a space he decided they were engaged in repairing and strengthening the stock pens.

"Hello! That's young Russ Cobb in charge down there, or I'm crazy." Though more curious than ever now, Pat's wariness increased. "If old Ben's figuring to take over T Square, that could be why he was so anxious to shuck me off," he pondered, frowning. "Does he think he can make anything like this stick?"

Turning over this unexpected development, he began for the first time to ask himself who had been the actual aggressor in the range fight so abruptly terminated by Pack Traver's death. All he had seen thus far had pointed a condemning finger straight at Traver himself; but Stevens had seen white become black before in these affairs. Resolving to dig as close to the bottom of this one as he could, he dismounted. Taking his time, he began to work down closer to the little ranch on foot.

There was no longer any doubt about young Cobb, he saw a few minutes later. Russ was unquestionably giving orders; and the three hands with him were carrying them out without question. Of Kip McKinley there was no sign whatever. Pat could not make out who the three range hands were, although he may have seen at least one of them at some time or other. They could be drifters that old Ben had picked up for a few weeks' work.

But ten minutes later, after crawling up a wash and working around for a close look at the brands on those waiting cow horses, Stevens stopped so sharply that he might have received a galvanic shock. His glance had picked up the bold outline of a War Ax burn on the nearest bronc. Sitting slowly back on his heels there in the wash, he rasped his lean jaw thoughtfully.

"War Ax, eh? What would that mean, now?"

Certainly it threw a clog into the smooth progress of his previous calculations. Chuck Stober's crew would be highly unlikely to take any part in renovating the broken-down T Square for Ben Cobb's benefit.

Studying the evidence minutely, Pat gravely shook his head. "My first guess goes plumb sour. So let's have another try at it." He touched his index finger lightly, as if counting. "Cobb's in a hurry to establish possession. So he hires anybody handy—including a horse thief who's just filled out his string at Chuck Stober's expense." Voicing this tentatively, he contemplated it with dissatisfaction. "No soap. Don't bullyrag me, Stevens! . . . Let's see." He frowned. "Russ needs horseflesh for extra hands, so he rented a few broncs from War Ax. . . . After Stober stood ready to let him get shot there in Ganado? Oh, shucks!" He caught himself up disgustedly. "Lay off, MacDuff. The least you can do, Mr. P. Stevens, Esq., is to watch and see what you shall see. I hope."

It was no pleasant prospect to watch a crew of corral menders while away the lengthy hours. But his luck was still good. Not twenty minutes after he had circled back to his horse Pat heard Russ Cobb calling brusque instructions to his men as he prepared to turn away. A moment afterward he strode into the yard and swung astride one of the broncs.

"Going somewheres?" Pat murmured alertly. "Good.

Who knows but I may manage to jog along with you, little man!"

He was, if the truth were known, much intrigued by this small adventure. Over the rugged years Stevens had learned to smell chicanery from miles off, and he smelled it now. There was something strictly not according to Hoyle in the arrangements going forward below him. He waited alertly to learn in what direction Russ Cobb would turn.

Russ started out of the T Square yard at a leisurely pace. For some minutes he did not seem intent on getting anywhere in particular. Watching, Pat was puzzled until it dawned on him that young Cobb was looking the ground over with a view to further improvements. Russ rode out to a point from which he could view the ranch. He glanced about, looking this way and that. Pat would have given a lot to know what was going through his busy mind.

"If Ben was planning to grab T Square, he'd use the range and let those buildings and pens go to pot," he told himself in some puzzlement. "Russ seems to have something far more ambitious in mind."

He found his opinion confirmed when Cobb turned away at last, starting across the range. It did not take long to guess his objective. He was making directly for the big War Ax spread.

Hanging back far enough to escape detection, Pat followed. If it was his thought that the young fellow could possibly be making for the Stober ranch for the purpose of reconnoitering, he soon learned different. Russ thrust on across the War Ax like a man who knew exactly what he was about; nor did it appear to concern him that he might run into any of Stober's punchers.

In a matter of minutes Stevens knew exactly how matters stood. "Why, Cobb is working for War Ax," he thought without surprise. "There can't be any two ways about it."

It was midday when Russ drew near the big main ranch. Chuck Stober was a material-minded man who went in for a display of prosperity. His ranch house was

a huge, sprawling adobe affair, and the complex of corrals and out-buildings was so extensive that on first
glance War Ax presented the appearance of a small vil-
age.

The similarity was further carried out by abundant activity about the place. Spirited horseflesh trotted the
length of the corrals, tossing bannerlike manes, and mules
grazed in a grassy pasture. Pigs and chickens populated
the lanes. Stober employed many Mexicans, whose shacks
made a snarl behind the ranch. The peons could be seen
working here and there; children and dogs made a noisy
hubbub somewhere in the background.

Never having done business with Stober, this was the
first time Pat had seen the place. Its imposing size and
activity opened his eyes. "Well, now! Stober likes to
play lord of the manor," he told himself. It was a broad
clue to the nature of the man—and Pat was rapidly becoming more interested.

Range hands were moving about, casually busy with
the chores of an extensive operation. Russ Cobb rode in
with a careless wave or two, and Pat saw at once that
a visitor on business would be likely to attract no particular attention here. Without ado he circled to come
in from a different direction, and approached the ranch
with bold confidence. As he expected, no one paid him
any heed. Riding into the yard that lay between the huge
adobe and the corrals, he spotted Russ Cobb's pony,
standing with reins dropped on the beaten ground.

Drawing up and slowly dismounting, he glanced swiftly
about. Mexican women were chattering at the rear of the
ranch house; men were at work in an adjacent horse pen.
Still no one seemed to have noted his arrival.

Cobb was nowhere in sight. Pat was not long in concluding, however, that he must have stepped into one or
another of the nearby tool shacks. He wanted a few words
with Russ in private and, as he started for the nearest
shed, he wondered what his luck would be this time.

It was better than good. Pausing at the open door of
the shed, he glanced in to find young Cobb inside. Russ
was kneeling on one knee, busily occupied in picking

over a box of rusty bolts. He glanced up as Pat's shadow fell on the floor, his expression faintly startled, with a slight tinge of chagrin. Russ got a grip on himself almost at once.

"You, Stevens? If I don't run into you in the danged-est places!" There was frank impatience in his tone. "What are you looking for here?"

"I might ask you that, boy." Pat gave him an easy grin. "Working, I take it? The last time I saw you, as I remember, you were hot and bothered about other things."

Cobb's glance darkened as he remembered. "You're talking about Pack Traver now. What I did," he thrust on half-defiantly, "I did for Pop. Jess Lawlor gave me a clean bill there in Ganado. There's no reason for you to bring it up now!"

Pat waved this away. "I'm not bringing anything up —except to say that, from what I saw myself, I agree fully with Lawlor," he assured. "I'm only surprised to find you working for War Ax now. What goes, if you don't mind saying?" he pursued calmly.

Young Cobb relaxed a bit. "I'm still trying to help Dad," he offered uncertainly. "Took the only job there was, to bring in a few dollars—if I have to spell it out for you—"

"You don't," said Pat quickly. "Ben'll be obliged for your help, and we both know it. . . . I thought I spotted you over on T Square an hour ago, Russ," he proceeded in a matter-of-fact tone. "Is Ben figuring on taking that range over, now that Traver won't be using it?"

Cobb glanced at him searchingly. "No such luck! It takes money to do such things, Stevens, and Pop has been hard hit already. . . . War Ax is moving in over there, as a matter of fact."

"That so?" Pat pretended a surprise he did not feel. "Don't Sheriff Lawlor have anything to say about it?"

"Oh, it's all legal and aboveboard," Russ assured cynically. "Stober's leased T Square from Traver's heirs— or his estate anyway—with an option to buy. I've been told off to see that it's fixed up as a range camp."

Pat nodded, musing shrewdly. It all sounded perfectly legitimate. With money behind them, the big ranchers could always do things that were beyond the reach of the little fellows. But for some reason, remembering Chuck Stober's icy indifference in Ganado, Pat did not like the looks of the thing. In the first place, he could not understand Russ Cobb's overlooking the big rancher's callousness and going to work for him under any circumstances.

Pat shook his head. "I was kind of hoping old Ben would get T Square," he allowed mildly. "Because you earned it, in a way. . . . I sort of planned to stop at Antler on the way home," he went on. "I will now. It can't do any harm to talk this whole deal over with Marty. The doc must be letting him talk a little by this time." He broke off, waiting for the answer.

Russ shook a stern negative, a stony look in his eyes. "You'll never talk it over with Marty, Stevens," he said tightly. "He can't talk—and he never will again. Marty died that same night, if you've got to know," he stated bleakly. "We kept it to ourselves this long. But that's the fact. So now yuh know."

Pat stared at him, astonished by this intelligence. But there could be no questioning Cobb's deadly seriousness.

"Good Lord! I certainly never heard that," Pat exclaimed, showing his deep concern. "It should've been reported right off!"

"No point in advertising it." Russ's gaze held his unflinchingly. "I can tell you now, Stevens. I sent word to Traver that I was looking for him. It wasn't an accident that we met in Ganado—no matter what he said. He knew what he had coming. He got it!"

[4]

Listening keenly, Pat found the young fellow's words too deliberate to be entirely credible. "Easy, Russ," he cautioned smilingly. "That practically amounts to a confession of murder, you know."

"How does it?" Cobb couldn't see it at all. "You were out there that day, Stevens! You know Traver killed Marty as well as I do." He spoke with belligerent force.

"No, I don't—and that's the whole point," reminded Pat shortly. "I know what you told me, Cobb, and no more. Jess Lawlor could give you plenty of trouble if he decided to look into this further."

"But you won't tell him?" Russ flashed warily.

"I won't have to if you do any more talking," Pat caught him up severely. "It looked plain enough there in Ganado that Pack was picking his own quarrel. Why not leave it at that? Are you bragging to me, or what?"

Russ denied any such intent. "Traver did his worst to smash us," he declared hoarsely. "There's no better proof that, with him out of the picture, all that has stopped." He was breathing hard now, his lips white. "What are you driving at anyhow, Stevens?"

Pat was still thinking about old Ben's suspicious brusqueness that morning. It did not seem as if he thought peace had been restored.

"Only that you and your dad still seem to have a chip on your shoulder," Pat replied mildly. "Is something bothering Ben now that you know of?"

Russ looked faintly alarmed. "You're—taking up my time, Stevens," he evaded hurriedly. "What could be?" He made an attempt to turn back to the box of bolts. But Stevens realized accurately enough that he had forgotten what he had been looking for.

"You don't even like to talk about it, do you?" Pat pressed him relentlessly.

"No. I don't!" Cobb showed a flash of returning spirit. "What is there to talk about? Marty's gone. It's all over and done. Haven't you got anything at all to do, Stevens?"

Perfectly aware that this offensive rudeness was designed to get rid of him, Pat gave over abruptly. Young and full of fire, Russ Cobb could be inflexibly stubborn. Convinced that silence was best, he would give out no further information—though he had already dropped more than he intended to.

Armed with the knowledge that Marty Cobb was dead, Pat resolved to return to Antler and face Ben Cobb for a showdown. It would not be impossible to break down his defenses. Pat was satisfied that both Cobbs were trying to hide something, and Ben might be tricked into talking.

"I gave you a piece of advice before, Cobb, that you didn't follow very closely. I'll do it again," he remarked, starting to turn away. "Take it easy, will you?"

"You take it easy," Russ shot back with rising antagonism. "I didn't ask for any of this, and I don't need any more of it! Is that clear?"

Paying no further heed, Stevens turned out of the shed. Cobb came outside a step or two, watching as he headed for his horse.

"Stevens."

A modulated, carrying voice came from across the yard. Looking up, Pat saw Chuck Stober regarding him. The rancher had stepped back out of the house at just the wrong moment. Although Pat never batted an eye, it was a nuisance running into the War Ax owner now that he had no further interests here.

Pat knew better than to show any appearance of beating a retreat. Turning that way easily, he moved toward the big rancher unhurriedly.

"Howdy, Stober. Fine place you have here."

Chuck was a large man, as broad across the shoulders as himself, and several inches taller. The sole sign of self-indulgence he allowed himself was that eternal cigar cocked in his square jaw.

"What brings you to War Ax, Stevens? Business, I expect," he grunted in his gravelly voice.

Thinking fast, Pat warily avoided this. "No, it happened to be a personal matter, Stober."

Chuck took his time in answering. Pat saw his glance travel to young Cobb and back again inquiringly. Was he mistaken in believing Stober had passed a discreet signal to someone beyond his line of vision?

"Sorry to hear that. I don't like my men bothered," Stober murmured.

"Oh, I'm leaving." As he replied Pat heard the scuffling footsteps of someone directly behind him. He glanced quickly around and saw two of Stober's War Ax hands approaching at a leisurely pace. While it might mean nothing, he did not like it. "If you're busy I'll get out from under, Stober—"

He was turning to face the advancing hands when, without any advance warning, a heavy blow caught him treacherously from behind. Too late he realized that turning his back on Chuck Stober was the worst mistake he could have made. There was time for that brief dismaying thought, and then blackness descended like a curtain over his reeling senses.

"Hey! That was fast action, boss," one of the hard-faced punchers exclaimed admiringly. He paused to look down at Steven's inert form slumped in a heap.

"Never mind the taffy, Deuce, I'm never slow. It'll pay you all to remember that," Stober rasped unemotionally. "Pick up that meddling fool, you two."

"Sure, boss. Sure." Deuce bent to hoist Stevens by his shoulders, while Rook Meara picked up his feet. "Where'll we drag him—?"

About to answer, Chuck paused to glance attentively toward Russ Cobb. Seeing Stevens ruthlessly slugged from behind, Russ took an impulsive step or two his way—only to halt.

"What about it, Cobb, any interest in this fellow?" Stober called across to him flatly.

Russ stood as if frozen, then shook his head slowly. "No, I didn't ask him here, Stober."

"Then get about your work—and forget that you ever saw him." The rancher made an authoritative gesture. "Get going, now."

After a deliberate pause, Cobb shrugged and turned away. Stober's were not the only eyes that watched this byplay. From a fringe of brush a couple of hundred yards away, where they crouched in the dust barely beyond detection at the edge of the ranch, Ezra and Sam Sloan had watched the treacherous assault on Stevens. They saw young Cobb start forward as if to come to Pat's aid, and then arrest himself, only to turn away at Stober's sharp order.

"What's the matter with him? Why don't the young fool break that up?" Sam gritted under his breath.

"For the same reason we don't," Ezra tossed back guardedly. "We're outnumbered here—and Cobb is smart enough to know it. Keep your pants on, will yuh? While we see what they do with Stevens—"

Pat had been wrong about more than one thing today. In passing the Bar ES range by a narrow margin on his way to Antler, he congratulated himself that once again he had avoided his crotchety friends, often a liability to him while engaged on a private errand.

He had in fact been seen by Ezra, who had hurried back to the little horse ranch to report the fact to Sam. Sloan was all for overtaking Stevens, or at least following him closely enough to learn where he might be bound. Accordingly they had set out, catching up in time to see Stevens in the midst of his talk with old Ben Cobb. The latter's unfriendly attitude, plus the rifle he carried, had warned them not to show themselves too soon.

Hanging back, they followed when Pat set off for T Square; and from their own point of vantage they saw and gathered as much there as he did. When he trailed Russ Cobb on to Stober's War Ax, they were not far behind. They saw him step into the tool shed after Cobb; and although they heard none of the talk they were still watching when Stevens emerged to be accosted by Stober himself, with totally unexpected results.

"Them lugs're haulin' Stevens off somewheres," Sam growled tensely, almost bursting his straining overalls in his excitement.

"Stober's pointin' to that other shack," seconded Ez, his single eye glued on the scene. "It's a grain shed, from the looks. . . . They're dumpin' him in there," he added, crouching to peer more alertly through the intervening brush.

As he said, Stevens was packed over to the shed, its door unlatched, and after his arms and legs were bound his unconscious form was tumbled inside carelessly. That done, the door was once more swung up and fastened.

"Dang little sense t' that—unless they're decidin' what to do with him." Sam was chewing his lips in vexation. "What'll we do now?"

Ez made up his mind swiftly. "No chance for us down there—if we could even reach it," he opined. "I'll stay here and watch while you take off. Get yourself to Ganado," he instructed, "and haul Lawlor's deputy out here by the heels or any way yuh have to!"

For once Sam was too thoroughly impressed by the urgency of the situation to scowl at his partner's officiousness. He started to crawl back toward the horses that they had concealed in a hollow, only to pause.

"Where'll I find yuh? Right here?" he queried in a hoarse whisper.

Ez showed crusty impatience. "It's Stevens I'm worryin' about," he rasped so harshly that Sloan was afraid they might be heard. "Get the law out here and head straight for the house—demand that Stober produce him! . . . I'll come runnin'," he promised, "the minute I spot yuh; and meanwhile if Pat's been moved I'll know it."

Sam grunted. Offering no further objections, he slithered away through the covering brush and was soon gone from sight.

Settling down to watch the War Ax yard, Ezra found it apparently peaceful once more, as if nothing had happened here. The grain shed into which Stevens had been thrown stood a little apart, and he could see it plainly. There was no sign of life anywhere about it.

Despite this deceptive calm Ezra watched so steadily that, twenty minutes later, it was a jolt to him to hear the faint thud of hoofs off at one side, and almost at once the rough voice of a man. "We ridin' to town to that dance tonight? Or are yuh still worryin' about the work?"

Crouching close against the mesquite clump behind which he had taken refuge, Ezra froze, turning his head very slowly. Through the brush he saw two range hands mounted on War Ax broncs. They were passing a matter of sixty feet away, making their way unhurriedly across the open range. Neither happened to look this way.

From their direction he did not think they would come across his horse hidden in a rocky hollow some distance behind him; yet at the same time every instinct in Ezra cried a warning. It was not safe for him to lie out in the brush, obviously spying on Stober's ranch, with that pair somewhere behind him. Leaving his post he started to make for his waiting pony, only to halt again.

"No, I ain't takin' the chance of their movin' Stevens," he growled bleakly, stubbornly turning back. "If they get me away from here they'll have to chase me!"

A quick glimpse of the ranch yard seemed to tell him that nothing had changed there. The passing riders were out of sight now; they had not spied him. He was safe for the moment. A sharp scrutiny of the grain shed, however, made him gulp. Was the door standing slightly ajar now—or was this a trick of his eyes? Gazing long, the lanky rawhide finally decided that such must be the case, and that Stevens was still penned in the place. Hadn't he seen the younger man securely bound with rope before being rolled in there?

After something like an hour of uneasy waiting, Ez began to give his attention to the open range surrounding the ranch. It seemed like the better part of another hour, and was probably fifteen minutes, before he picked up two swiftly riding figures advancing across the swells from the direction of Ganado.

"Sam and that deputy." He nodded to himself, although they were yet too tiny to make out with any distinctness. Ten minutes later he was sure of Sloan's rotund figure and short legs jutting beyond the barrel of his bronc. The second rider made him stop and squint to see better. "That's not Lawlor's deputy," he brought out explosively. "Better yet—it's Lawlor himself! Sam must've stumbled onto him in town. Now I reckon we'll get some action!"

Watching alertly, he waited in concealment until the pair drew close. Hurrying then for his own mount, he swung up and headed straight for War Ax. No one obstructed his path, and he was able to jog into the ranch yard at just about the time that Sam and the sheriff rode in.

The partners met with partially lifted hands, a tacit signal perfectly understood by both. Sheriff Lawlor looked at Ezra soberly without speaking. Sam raised his eyebrows in inquiry. Ez shook his head curtly.

"No change," he muttered gruffly. "He's still in there."

Lawlor absorbed this, his rocky face emotionless. From his sober expression he seemed to be storing up a lecture for Stevens once he caught up with him. Long since he had figured out in his plodding way that Stevens was interesting himself in things which did not concern him. Without comment he turned directly toward the big War Ax house.

"Stober," he called out heavily, reining up at the back door. "Are yuh there?"

Mexican women could be seen scuttling about, and range hands stared at Lawlor from the corrals, but it was several minutes before Stober himself put in an appearance, lounging to the door from somewhere within and pausing with his thick shoulder braced against its frame.

"Well. This is an honor, Sheriff!" Sarcasm tinged his rumbling voice, and he did not seem at all alarmed by the unexpected visit. "What can I do for you?"

His mock humility said that he doubted there could be anything. But Lawlor soon disillusioned him. "You can trot Stevens out here, mister. And do it pronto!"

"Stevens? Stevens?" Chuck weighed the name in masterly mystification. "You must mean that Lazy Mare man. What would I know about him, Lawlor?"

"Yuh ought to be able to guess! Sloan here swears yuh slugged him and put him away."

"*I* slugged him—?" Stober put on an expression of tolerant incredulity. "Oh, come now! Don't tell me you believe any such falderal, Sheriff!"

"Yes—yuh slugged Stevens, and I saw yuh do it!" charged Sam bitterly. "What's more, Stober, yuh know only too well where he is right now!"

"I do." Chuck was dangerously composed. "In that case, maybe you can refresh my mind—"

"Pat's in that grain shed yonder, Lawlor." Sloan pointed. "Because I saw him tossed in there, and Ez says he ain't come out."

Stober gazed from one to the other admiringly. "Real smart, aren't we?" he murmured. "Why don't you just go over there and look, Lawlor?" he invited carelessly. "Maybe that'll satisfy these—ah—busybodies."

The same thought occurred to Ezra and Sam simultaneously. "Watch it, Jess!" Sam barked. "This may be a set-up for the same thing to happen to all three of us!" He shot a suspicious look about the yard, drawing his gun in readiness for anything. Ezra followed suit.

Stober's answer was a scornful laugh. "Sorry to see you a victim of such horseplay, Lawlor," he sneered indulgently. "While they're playin' cowboys and Indians, shall we go over and have a look in that shed? I don't rightly remember being in there myself for weeks," he elaborated easily.

Lawlor doggedly dismounted and headed that way, and Stober followed at a more leisurely pace. Drawn after them despite his wariness, Sam stayed on his horse. He kept a sharp eye on the wily rancher as Lawlor reached the door of the shed and started to open it. As a consequence he was the first to hear the lawman's exclamation of discovery.

Lawlor swung the door wide, and turned to glare at

Ezra. "What's the meanin' of this, Ez?" he roared. "I don't see hide nor hair of Stevens here! Nor nobody else!"

Unbelieving, Sam crowded his mount close to peer in over their heads. It was perfectly true. Except for a few feed sacks in the corners, the shed was empty

[5]

When he was thrown to the ground to be tied before being tossed into the grain shed, Pat Stevens was jarred to partial consciousness. Although too dazed to open his eyes, he caught a brief scuff of boots and diminishing voices which at first conveyed no meaning to his senses.

Then suddenly his wits sprang awake. It came back to him swiftly what had happened. Too wary to betray himself, he lay inert. But although he kept his body slack as ropes were looped about his ankles and knees, and his hands were drawn behind his back and bound there, he saw to it that the loops could not be drawn as tight as his captors thought them.

"Hurry it up and get him out of sight, will you?" he heard Chuck Stober's terse order.

A moment later he was tumbled unceremoniously through the shed door. He waited after hearing the door rasp shut to make sure he had been left alone here. Through slitted eyes he glanced about without moving.

Cracks between the boards afforded a dim light, if not enough space to see what went on outside. But receding footsteps and ensuing silence assured him he had been abandoned to his pen. An experimental trial of his bound wrists said that his strategem had probably been successful. There was play in the bonds, and that was all he needed. After five minutes of trying he got one hand free; and it was not much longer before he could stand up cautiously, the ropes dropping from his legs.

All the while his mind was working busily with the problem of Stober. He could not understand why the rancher had thought such a course necessary. Did he have something to conceal which he thought Stevens had already discovered? The only answer within easy reach was the fact that War Ax was taking over T Square.

"Cobb told a straight story," he mused thoughtfully. "Whatever the true facts, Russ believes Stober took a lease with the option to buy. But maybe Stober lied to him about that."

It was a cue to be followed up if he ever succeeded in wriggling out of this tight pinch.

Picking up his hat, which had been kicked inside after him, Pat tucked the rope bonds out of sight. Then he turned to the question of what could be seen from this shed. A glimpse through the widest crevice on one side showed him a partial view of the yard. Other cracks revealed even less; and on one side, toward the house, he could see nothing at all.

As nearly as he could judge he had been left strictly alone here in the grain shed. For how long? Only as long as it took Stober to decide what disposal would be made of his case, he realized, and that might come soon. He had no great length of time in which to settle on his own course of action.

The thought took him quickly back to the slab door. While it had been fastened on the outside, it did not fit very snugly in its frame. He could make out the wooden turn-button. Picking up a short piece of baling wire from the floor, he straightened it out in his fingers and inserted it through the crack. Only a moment's manipulation served to turn the button, and the door sagged open slightly.

Pat paused there, thinking it over swiftly. He was free. Dared he slip out of this flimsy prison and make a break for the open range—or was the shed being watched?

Carefully thrusting the door open a bare inch, he peered cautiously out. From here he could see a part of the yard and the corrals. Men were working ponies in a pen some distance away, while a couple more sat on the fence and watched. There appeared to be no interest whatever in the grain shed. Nor was Chuck Stober anywhere in sight.

Pat let the door drift shut while he thought it over again briefly. He was not long in reaching a decision. There was everything to gain in making an attempt to break away at once, and little to lose. Pulling his hat down firmly, he paused for an instant at the door; then with firm decision he thrust it open and stepped out.

If a guard was posted at one corner of the shed, squatted with his back to the wall, he did not appear. Instead of turning directly away, Stevens struck out across the yard at a leisurely pace. From the shed door he had spotted three saddled broncs standing hip-shot in a corner of the yard. It was toward these that he headed, keeping his head down and looking neither to the right nor left.

He was certainly seen. Out of the corner of his eye he noted heads turning this way, over there at the corral. But the hands did not immediately identify him, for a simple reason on which he had calculated. Those who had watched Stober slug him had last seen him with his Stetson flying off. They must have calculated that he would be out cold for the better part of an hour at least. He was dressed much like any other range hand; and at his unhurried pace, with his hat cocked forward at a jaunty angle, they took him without question for one of the many War Ax hands moving about the place.

Shooting a look ahead, Pat saw that he was near the tethered broncs. Not yet had anyone started forward to head him off. It was a relief to step in between the ponies, into partial cover. But he was not safe here for longer than a minute or two. Swiftly choosing what looked like the strongest and fastest horse that fortunately also had a more or less nondescript color, he tugged the tie rope free and backed it away from the rack.

It was the work of only a second to swing lithely astride. Starting the bronc across the yard toward a lane leading toward the open range, Stevens was able partially

ly to hide his face by bending over and pretending to
fumble with his stirrup strap. He reached the lane safely
and had to restrain himself from raking the bronc into
a quickened pace.

Yet his spirits rose sharply. A dozen yards more and
he would be in the clear. Still no one raced this way to
cut him off. Incredibly, by his very boldness he had succeeded in winning clear without the necessity to fight
through a ring of determined enemies.

Risking a glance back as he rode clear of the lane into
the open brush, Pat could not detect any evidence that
his escape was noted at all. He breathed deeply.

"Let that be a lesson, Stevens—and you can be glad
Ez and Sam will never know how much of a fool you
made of yourself today," he murmured humorously to
himself. "At least I'll be primed for Stober the next time
we meet. And the sooner that is, the better it'll suit me!"

Seeing that his progress remained unnoted, he struck
off across War Ax range, losing no time in putting a ridge
between himself and the ranch. Even here he was uneasy. It would be decidedly awkward if he should run
into one of Stober's punchers on the fellow's own home
ground. Should he meet a band of them, they would not
hesitate to employ such measures as they thought called
for.

"I better get over to Ganado and lose myself fast," he
murmured.

Heading that way, he avoided at least one group of
War Ax hands without difficulty. It was due entirely to
his careful vigilance that, half an hour later, he spotted
two riders racing his way at a rapid pace.

Prudence drove him promptly into thick mesquite that
still allowed him to glimpse the hurrying pair briefly as
they passed. What he saw caused his mouth to drop
open. For a brief space he was unable to comprehend.

"Wha-at? Sam Sloan and Jess Lawlor—making at top
speed for War Ax! Now what would be the meaning of
that?"

He was quick enough to put two and two together.
That runt must have seen what happened there in

Stober's yard after all," he told himself with a rueful grin. "It wouldn't surprise me at all if Ezra's still over there watching—and meanwhile Sam picked up Lawlor in Ganado and brought him along."

The thought of what would happen if Sam or Ezra knew about the grain shed and believed him still inside made his grin widen impishly.

"This I've got to see."

Turning his horse back, he rode after the hurrying pair without any real effort to overtake them. He hung back at a distance, seeing Sloan and the lawman ride boldly on into War Ax. Since he was unable to see the yard clearly, Pat thought it best not to crowd his good fortune, retiring instead to a rocky ledge crest several hundred yards above the surrounding range, from whence he could obtain a clear view.

It was about twenty minutes before anything happened. Then he saw a trio of riders coming away from Stober's ranch, no longer hastening now. It was not difficult to recognize all three of them. As he had shrewdly guessed, Ezra was one. He appeared to be arguing hotly with Sheriff Lawlor, and Sam was putting in an occasional word. They were obviously coming away empty-handed, a fact which none appeared to relish.

Pat watched their progress without riding out to join them. "Well! I can't keep my troubles secret any longer," he reflected. "The most I can do is to keep those birds puzzled for a while." Turning his bronc away, he made for the Lazy Mare on a course calculated not to cross that of the others.

Reaching home by midafternoon, Stevens went about his work without comment to anyone. His foreman Zeke Johnson, and Crusty Hodge, the grizzled, aging and crabbed handyman, were used to Pat's frequent absence, and they made no reference to it today. Glancing out the kitchen door as he placed his employer's supper on the table, Hodge only growled disgustedly.

Pat had heard hoofs pounding outside in the yard. "Who is that, Crusty?" he inquired without looking up from his plate.

"Who would it be but that Ezra, always ready to mooch a free meal!" Hodge was far from partial to Ezra, who paid him scant attention; and he lost no opportunity to reveal as much.

"Tell him to come in." Pat ignored the old man's habitual grumpiness.

Despite orders, all Crusty would consent to do was to hold the screen door open part way and look at Ezra. The lanky tracker read the grudging invitation accurately enough. Tethering his bronc, he made for the kitchen porch and clumped briskly up the steps.

"Come in, Ez," called Stevens in a hearty welcome. "I kind of looked for you all day. Why didn't you bring Sam?"

Halting just inside the door while he assured himself of Pat's presence here, Ezra opened his mouth and shut it again. "Dang you, Stevens! You're too cute to live," he burst out hardly at length, injured accusation in his tone.

"What's that?" Pat looked up in surprise, obviously waiting for the other to proceed.

"Never mind the smoke screen! I seen Stober slug yuh and then toss yuh into that shed! Did yuh burrow out of there like a mole, or what?"

Turning away from the table, Pat squared around to face him. "Know about that, do you?" He grunted. "And you mean you hung around and never made a move to help me——?" He threw what severity he could muster into his voice.

For a second Ezra appeared about to explode. Barely in time he caught the twinkle in Pat's eyes. "Oh, shucks." Moving forward, he sank into a chair and turned to survey Crusty Hodge offensively. "Where's my coffee?" he roared.

Breathing fire, Hodge managed to slop steaming coffee into a cup and bang it down before him. Winking solemnly at Stevens while he stirred, Ez settled back.

"How did you work it, boy?"

"Stupid as it sounds, Ezra, I untied myself, walked out and borrowed a bronc, and rode away." Grinning, Pat related exactly how it had been done. "Where were you?"

Vague as he sounded about his reason for being there, Ez told how he and Sam had witnessed Stober's treachery, and how he had sent Sam to Ganado while he remained to watch. "But I swear I never seen yuh walk out of there." Elaborating, Ez recalled the two War Ax hands who had nearly flushed him from his post. "Dang 'em, they must have drew my attention away for just long enough!"

Pat nodded. "I probably stepped out at just about the time you were ducking them. I sure didn't make myself conspicuous." He leaned forward interestedly. "What happened there at Stober's, anyhow?"

Growing red about the gills, the one-eyed man told about the clash with Chuck Stober. "He was cool as a cucumber about it all—and now Jess Lawlor's convinced I'm no better than a fool." He snorted. "I don't think he even believes it happened, Stevens!"

"Take it easy, Ezra. I'll fix that."

"How will yuh fix it?" challenged the other.

Pat spread his hands. "Easy. If you want to see it done, just stick around till morning. Results guaranteed." He grinned.

He would add no more, but Ezra needed little to persuade him to remain overnight at the Lazy Mare. They discussed the War Ax owner's object without getting anywhere.

"Stober will bear watching," Pat concluded sagely at the end. "He stepped way outside the law, and there must be a reason. Time will tell." He paused. "How in the world did you arrange to have Jess Lawlor out there so fast?"

"Didn't. I sent Sam after Lawlor's deputy—and the first person he ran into there in Ganado was Jess himself. That satisfy yuh?"

Sleeping late for them, the pair got up at dawn, and after a leisurely breakfast set out for Dutch Springs. Once there Stevens appeared to have no pressing chore. They racked their broncs and walked down to the post office in Winters' store, where they stood around to wait for the mail.

It was not long before an acquaintance called Ezra aside. Pat scarcely noticed, although he kept a watch on the street. Presently he saw what he was watching for. Stepping outside, he started up the plank sidewalk with apparent unconcern, and a moment later came face to face with Sheriff Lawlor. It could be no accident that Chuck Stober was with Jess at the moment. After losing his prisoner so promptly, the wily rancher had hurried to Lawlor to mend his fences.

"Howdy, Jess." Nodding, Stevens started to pass on.

"Hold on here, Stevens!" The lawman spoke authoritatively, quickly barring his way.

Looking up in surprise, Pat halted. "Yes—?"

"Let me get this straight." Eyeing him sharply, Jess began to breathe hard. "Were you slugged and held over at War Ax, Stevens, or weren't you?"

"Oh, nonsense!" Stober interrupted swiftly, in a tone of superior tolerance. "Can't you read the earmarks of a crazy story yet, Lawlor?"

Jess paid him no attention whatever, waiting pointedly for Pat's answer.

"Me?" Pat was able to pretend easy ignorance of the matter. "You see me here, Lawlor," he fenced smoothly, avoiding the impulse to glance at Stober. "Who have you been listening to, anyhow?"

"That's right, Stevens—don't lie," Stober caught him up dryly. "I tried to tell Lawlor nobody would be spending time over at my place unless he had business there. Be smart—just stay strictly away from War Ax," he addressed Pat directly, a thin warning in his inflection. "Before something does happen to you!"

Pat laughed, believing he found something like chagrin in the man's stern sobriety. "That's fair warning at any rate," he allowed carelessly. "You heard him, Jess. It's not healthy to go sifting around War Ax without an iron-clad reason."

Stober was willing to let it ride that way. "I always like to know what's going on," he murmured. "I expect to get talked about. Any big man does. What I didn't expect was a responsible man like Lawlor here to take such claptrap seriously."

"Well, I was told about this business and I had to look into it." Taking Pat's apparent denial at face value, Lawlor showed dogged disgust. "I intend to go into it deeper, Stober, if I find any shadow of reason why I should."

"Go ahead." Chuck grunted briefly. "But just remember, Sheriff, I'm a taxpayer too. I can vote you out just as fast as I helped vote you in. There's always that to think about!"

Turning on his heel as he spoke, and favoring Lawlor with a sour smile in which there was also a triumphant challenge, Stober coolly walked away. It did not escape Pat what he was about. In leaving these two men together, Stober was confidently defying them to compare notes about him. His brazen self-assurance could not have been made plainer.

[6]

"So what am I to believe now, Stevens?" asked the sheriff sourly. He stood straight and firm, waiting for the other to speak.

Ezra came striding up as they stood there, urgency in his manner. "Say, boy—I just spotted that Stober a minute or two ago," he burst out portentously. "Are yuh aimin' to do somethin' about him?"

Pat looked from him to Lawlor, then shrugged. "I can tell you now, Jess. Stober did slug me and tie me up, there on War Ax," he said levelly. "But what can we do about it? I don't intend to fuss around with any such petty charge—and I don't need to tell you that Stober would just laugh off a stiff warning."

Lawlor looked disgusted. "Hang it! Why didn't yuh talk that way ten minutes ago?" he exclaimed gruffly. "If you mean that Stober can bluff me and get away with it, I'll be the judge of that!"

Pat only smiled. "When I hand you anything at all on that gent, I'll be dead sure of it, Jess."

Lawlor vehemently waved this aside. "Pah! . . . You're the fast talker, Stevens. In all fairness I just can't believe any of this now. Stober *said* he was bein' talked about. Yuh don't give me a shred of evidence to go on!"

Winking at Ezra, Pat half-turned away, motioning to the lawman to follow. Reluctantly complying, Lawlor did not know what to expect until Pat reached the hitch rack at which he and Ezra had tied up their mounts half an hour ago. While Lawlor watched, Pat stripped his saddle off, swinging it over the bar. He turned the animal then, before removing the bridle, and Lawlor abruptly comprehended, seeing the War Ax brand on its flank.

"There you are. That's the bronc I was riding yesterday, Jess, after I lost my own," Pat told him dryly. He slapped the horse on the flank and watched it trot off up the street. "Unless Stober catches it, it'll go on home now." He grinned blandly at Lawlor. "Does that help?"

Jess pretended anger. "I asked what happened to you, right in front of Stober! You're mighty highhanded in your dealings with the law," he brought out tartly.

"*I* am! Then what do you say about our friend Stober—if we're getting down to the fine points?"

Lawlor looked as if he could have found plenty to say. Instead he swung on his heel and strode off, his jaw outthrust. Ezra looked after him with a mixture of shrewdness and contempt.

"Why, he's mad because yuh did come up with proof of your story by showin' him that horse," he muttered. "I don't believe he wanted any real evidence against Stober—because now he'll be forced to do somethin' about it!"

Pat nodded agreement. "Like everybody else, Jess hates to be asked to use his brains. He knows dealing with Chuck Stober won't turn out any picnic." He thought about it briefly, leaning against the hitch rail. "To get down to cases, Ez, what *have* we got against Stober, exactly?"

"What do yuh mean?" Ezra looked suspicious. "In my book we got enough to hang him—"

Pat ignored this. "Let's look at it again," he urged. "We know he's anxious enough to keep strangers off his spread to tap me on the head. What for? I didn't hear any talk about tossing me in the wash or any such thing. For all we know he might have turned me loose in an hour."

"Nice to think so anyhow." Ezra sneered at the likelihood.

"Anyway, nothing much happened," Pat proceeded, brushing off his misadventure lightly.

"So why did it happen at all?" argued Ez. "That's the main point, Stevens. And yuh ain't answered it."

"I know." Pat had been puzzling over the answer for twenty-four hours. "Something's up. Is it that deal over on T Square, or something we haven't got wind of yet?"

Sam came jogging into town while they were batting it around. Spotting them, the little man dismounted to join them. "It's a wonder yuh wouldn't let a feller know yuh was all right," he greeted Stevens offensively.

"I am," Pat answered briefly. "The question is, what were you doing wandering around War Ax without permission?" he retorted with some curtness. "Don't you know you're liable to get into trouble over there?"

Sloan looked astonished for a second. Then he flashed a comprehending grin. "Yuh pulled a fast one on us, boy—not to mention Stober," he commented admiringly. "What did go on over there, if a man can ask?"

Pat filled him in briefly. After conning the situation for a moment they resumed the discussion of the War Ax owner. Sam was convinced that Stober sought to conceal illegal activities of some nature. "He couldn't be this beef stealer, could he?" he queried alertly.

Pat did not even consider it. "That stopped altogether with Pack Traver's finish," he pointed out tersely.

"Did it?" inserted Ezra shrewdly. "Are yuh sure of that? Did old Ben Cobb tell yuh so, or what?"

Stevens scowled at them. "The trouble with you two, you don't think big," he declared scornfully. "Stober might steal a county—or the Dutch Springs bank. A steer or two wouldn't interest him."

"Then what about T Square? Is that big enough?" Ezra asked.

Pat nodded slowly. "It might be—and it's the only thing I can think of right off," he admitted. "The trouble there is that Russ Cobb told me Stober leased the place fair and square—"

"Cobb told yuh!" Sam's tone was derogatory. "Stood right there and watched yuh get slugged, didn't he? And did he make a move to help?"

Pat turned that over. "He didn't—for the same reason you weren't able to, probably," he returned finally. Yet he was impressed. "It could be a mistake to take Russ at face value, at that. I can't forget that he turned up working for Stober. But we can plug that hole without any trouble," he added after a pause.

"How so?"

"Can I ask you two to keep an eye on Stober there at T Square for a week or so?" Pat asked. "I suspect I may be watched myself. But you two will be safe enough."

After some token reluctance, the leathery pair assented. "Yuh don't want us to do anything, though, or show ourselves?" Sam inquired.

"No, let's not tip Stober off that anybody's interested in him," was the reply. "Because he can afford to wait until we get tired of that. Then we'll have to start all over again."

After more talk the Bar ES partners set off. Pat rode home in the ranch wagon with Crusty Hodge, who had driven in today for supplies. He was not surprised to learn that his own bronc, abandoned at War Ax in his hasty escape, had been found on the range, reins trailing, still bearing its saddle. Stober had in turn released the horse to wander home as it would, as Pat had done in town.

On the following day no word came from his crotchety friends. But late Friday afternoon Sam Sloan rode in to report. Stevens met him in the Lazy Mare yard.

"What luck, Samuel?" he queried.

Sam dismounted, giving him a straight look. "Stober's takin' full charge over at T Square, and no mistake," he declared. "Young Cobb's crew has started tearin' down the old buildings. Stevens, and Stober himself was over there this morning. I thought yuh ought to know."

Pat nodded. "No longer any mistake about it, eh? Did you see anything else at all?"

"Ain't that enough?" Sam looked offended. Pat's response was a chuckle.

"Just asking," he assured. "If Stober's gone that far it must be on the level." He pondered briefly. "It's a shame *he* should benefit from all that range, though, after the Cobbs went to the trouble of eliminating Traver—"

Sam looked startled. "Say, that's right! Yuh don't suppose . . ." But he did not pursue this further. "What do yuh want me and Ez to do now, Stevens?"

Pat was undecided. "I'll inquire around here in town," he returned. "But as near as I can see, we haven't got a thing yet that we can touch Stober with. I know you've got your own work to do. Why don't you and Ezra forget it for a while?"

"If yuh say so. Seems like it's quittin' with the job half-done, though," Sam grumbled. "But you're the doctor."

He stayed for an hour and then left. For several days Stevens was busily engaged in gathering a sale herd, delivery to be made on his own range. Though he enjoyed the work, it left little time for speculation of any sort. As usual with him, he put the immediate job behind him before turning to other things. Early the following week, however, he found occasion to ride in to the Powder County land office, a little shack on the edge of Dutch Springs. Pat knew the land agent, Martin Kramer.

"Well, Stevens! Don't tell me you're thinking about

taxes already," Kramer observed facetiously, looking up from his desk as Pat stepped in the door.

"I like to think ahead, Mart," was the latter's non-committal response. He chatted with the man for a few minutes before getting down to business. Even now he did not see any point in revealing to Kramer exactly what was on his mind.

"I'm always willing to add a few acres to Lazy Mare for winter range," he said finally. "And I got to thinking about Pack Traver's old place. With him gone now it could be lying idle. What is the status of T Square, any-how?"

"Well, let's see." Putting on his professional manner, Kramer turned to the records. "You may not have heard that Charles Stober leased out there, with an option to buy—"

"That so?" Pat left it at that, waiting.

Kramer came up with a batch of papers, glanced through them briefly, and nodded. "I remember now. We got notice last week that Stober was taking up his option. Here it is, here." He waved a paper. "I'm afraid you're too late, Stevens. It seems a bit early, I know. But a man can't waste time on these things."

Pat thanked him. He had all he needed to know. Talking a few minutes longer, on the pretense of being interested in any available rangeland, he presently left.

He walked up the street slowly, thinking it over. There could be no question now that the War Ax owner was openly buying T Square. Everything appeared to be in order; but at the same time Pat was not altogether satisfied.

"I wonder if there could be any phony legal angle here?" he said to himself, pausing in the street. "Kramer wouldn't tip me off if there was. But Judge Jeff would probably know."

He turned down toward the Red Men's Hall, and was climbing the outside stairway when he halted briefly to glance along the street, eyes slitted. An elderly man standing on the corner by the bank had caught his attention. It was the first time in months that he had seen old Ben Cobb in Dutch Springs.

"I'll tackle him once more, soon as I get done with Blaine," he decided.

Judge Blaine had occupied second-floor quarters in the old frame building for a number of years. Dignified and authoritative, the jurist was sometimes out on circuit. But retiring as he preferred to remain in his capacity as a private citizen, he was always available to old friends when at home. He answered Pat's knock and greeted him with a level stare.

"Come in, boy. What's your problem this time?" he asked in a rumbling voice that was rather startling, coming from his small frame.

"Howdy, Judge. I just stopped by to swap range gossip," Pat grinned, waiting till Blaine stiffly seated himself, then following suit.

Judge Jeff grunted skeptically. "All right—out with it. What particular piece of gossip do you think I ought to know better than you do, Stevens?"

Pat sobered. "I'm on a fishing expedition, Judge," he admitted. "This may not amount to anything. But I like to know." Proceeding quietly, he reminded the jurist of Pack Traver's death, and described Chuck Stober's manner of taking over T Square. "He's certainly not hiding anything," he admitted, explaining that a War Ax crew was tearing down the old buildings and repairing the corrals.

"I know." Judge Blaine had already heard the news. "What makes you feel there's anything unusual in that?" he asked shrewdly.

"Nothing, on the face of it," Pat conceded. "Kramer told me down at the land office just now that Stober leased with an option to buy—and then took up his option. . . . But let me tell you a little story, Judge."

Blaine listened attentively to Pat's tale of his attempt to interest himself in the tangled affairs of the Cobbs. "I expect we all figured Pack Traver was trying to chase them off and grab Antler for himself," he summed up.

"But what's the result? Chuck Stober steps in and takes over."

The jurist chuckled dryly. "That's happened before," he observed. "Big ranchers are all apt to be out of the same basket, boy—no matter where they started from at the bottom."

"Sure. But listen to this." Pat told how he had traced Russ Cobb to War Ax, where he now worked, and how the owner had reacted to his visit. "Has he got something to hide?" he broke off, glancing across keenly. "And what is it?"

Blaine alertly questioned him about every aspect of his adventure. He weighed Pat's account of last week's meeting, and considered it briefly. Finally he shook his white head. "Stober's arrogant and overbearing," he ruled, not hiding a natural indignation. "But I can't see that all this has anything to do with his taking over T Square. That seems legal and shipshape to me, Stevens. Unless you could prove coercion of Traver's heirs," he added.

Pat had no intention of trying. "I don't even know who they are," he admitted. "But Judge, I don't like it at all. With two killings clearing the way for Stober's piece of luck—Marty Cobb's and Traver's—the whole deal smells to high heaven. You won't deny that?"

Blaine didn't. "Still it *may* be coincidence," he insisted. "Stranger things have happened. . . . Hang either one of those killings on Stober, boy, and then I'll listen."

They talked longer without any materially different result. Judge Jeff had only one piece of advice to offer.

"I don't like Stober's highhandedness any better than you do," he declared. "But if you hope personally to keep out of trouble, Stevens, stay away from his place and stay away from him. If he's playing fast and loose with the law, as these stories seem to indicate, he'll tip his hand sooner or later. No reason for you to be involved in the smashup."

"None at all—except that I'd like a heap to trigger it," returned Pat frankly. "But I'll remember what you say, Judge." He got up. "Thanks for your time anyway."

Blaine had further prudent comments to make, but, as he descended the stairs to the street after leaving the old man, Pat remained unconvinced. "Of course in his capacity Judge Jeff can only act on ironclad evidence," he mused. "And that influences his manner of thinking. Maybe that's what he was trying to tell me all along."

Taken altogether, the result of the conference was not much different from what Pat had expected. Never yet had the forces of law and order gone out of their way to solve a puzzling mystery, where no crime was immediately apparent.

"And that's the answer to whether I can forget about Stober or not," he thought soberly. "Let him off this time, and next thing I know he'll be gnawing away at Lazy Mare."

It was not the first time he had had a bear by the tail, unable to let go. He was painstakingly considering his course of action as he moved upstreet toward the post office, when an interruption occurred.

The high-pitched tones of a cracked and querulous voice struck his ear, and glancing up he saw two old-timers facing each other across the street in front of the Gold Eagle. Pat unconsciously hurried his pace. One of the pair was old Ben Cobb—and the other, he noted with something like apprehension, was Crip Colcord, owner of the Saw Buck, which adjoined both Antler and War Ax in the southern end of Powder Valley.

Obviously Cobb had a bone to pick with his neighbor, for he was waving a bony fist and shouting imprecations. The next instant Pat sucked in his breath as Ben sprang forward to attack the other man bodily. Old Crip was lame, and this sort of thing could not be allowed to go on. A cry went up.

Leaping forward, Pat was the first to reach the two. Grasping Cobb firmly by the shoulder and hurling him back, Stevens stepped in between the pair, forcing a cessation of hostilities.

"Now. What's going on here, anyhow?"

Cobb paid the least possible amount of attention, his craggy face knotted with rage. He could not ignore Pat altogether. "Stand aside, Stevens, and let me get at that robber!" he fumed.

Despite his handicap—one leg was shorter than the other, so that he hobbled precariously when he moved —old Crip was ready to tangle pugnaciously with the Antler owner. At the same time he was frankly bewildered.

"Tell me what we're fightin' about, yuh old fool," he roared, glaring at Ben savagely. "At least I like t' know why I've got to flatten yuh!"

"Don't play dumb, Colcord!" Cobb bellowed indignantly. "Just keep your cows back off my grass—and I don't mean part of the time either!"

"Oh hell." Crip was blisteringly scornful. "There's that moth-eaten old complaint again! My cows couldn't be driven onto your range, yuh blithering lunkhead. My graze is so much better than yours—"

Cobb made a violent gesture, his congested features nearly black. "That excuse may go over here in town," he retorted fiercely. "But my boy Russ has been watchin' yuh, Colcord. He saw the whole thing!"

Colcord made an awkward attempt to rush him bodily. Again Pat stepped in in time to keep the belligerent old rawhides apart. Forced back against his will, Crip glowered at his neighbor, breathing fire. "What did yuh see?" he challenged.

"My boy saw your stove-up old puncher driftin' Saw Buck stuff across the Antler line," blared Cobb flatly. "It ain't no secret that you hired Kip McKinley after Traver went under! I happen to know McKinley's achin' for the chance to get back at Antler—and you knowed it too, Colcord. That's why you hired him!"

To Stevens the charge sounded particularly ominous, the circumstances altogether too pat. It was in just such a manner that the feud between Pack Traver and the Cobbs had commenced. Was this the prelude to another range grab?

Colcord himself was not impressed. "Pah," he spat out. "Yuh had to dig deep for that yarn, mister. Kip McKinley would like nothin' better than never to hear your name again—or Antler's either. But he takes orders from me and minds his business." He put on a quizzical expression. "What is it you're after, anyhow?"

"That's right! Try to make a fool of me!" old Ben bleated, livid with fury. "It's been tried before—but you crooks never learn. . . . I'll learn yuh. Fast!" he wound up vindictively.

Before anyone divined his intent he yanked his six-gun out of the leather and threw it up. Barely in time Pat caught the move. *"Here—!"* He leaped forward, batting at the gun at no little risk to himself. It crashed harmlessly, the shot deflected into the air.

Cobb attempted to stumble aside out of Pat's reach and try again. Stevens whirled after him with pantherlike speed. With a single wrench he wrested the gun from Ben's grasp.

"Watch what you're doing, old man. If you think you have an honest grievance, take it to Jess Lawlor," he advised severely, breaking the Colt and shaking the shells into his palm. "Don't treat us to any more such work or you'll wind up in a real jam."

A snort was Cobb's only answer. Clearly he thought himself among enemies here in town. Nursing his wrist, he glared from Pat to Colcord and back again. From his expression it was plain that he was by no means cowed.

"Shall we go to Lawlor right now and settle this?" Pat barked at him.

"No." Only the vehemence of Ben's tone was subdued. "Maybe I—was a mite hasty there, Stevens. But listenin' to all them barefaced lies made me see red."

Pat weighed his cooling anger and handed the gun back. "You're entitled to your opinion, old-timer. But go slow about calling names," he advised tersely. "Even if you're sure, you'll have to produce proof before it will justify pulling a gun on another man. . . . Did you ever know Colcord to grab your grass before?" he pressed sharply.

Cobb delayed a second before answering. "That's got nothin' to do with it," he evaded then grudgingly. "He's doin' it now, but he won't get away with it! I know how to bide my time when I have to!"

Crip Colcord was listening in incredulous silence, and even Pat became disgusted with such stubbornness. "That'll be about enough." He spoke decidedly. "You can pack out of here, Cobb, before you find yourself explaining to the sheriff how come you lost your head. Lively now!"

Muttering angrily, Ben thrust the empty Colt in its sheath and turned away. If looks could kill, Colcord would have dropped on the spot. Instead he turned to Pat with a crooked smile, as Cobb shuffled off down the street.

"I suppose I ought t' thank yuh, Stevens," said old Crip ruefully. "Somehow I'd rather've tangled with that catamount and settled it here and now. The way it is it'll just drag along, and I'll have this all to go through again!"

"Think so?" Pat pretended unconcern. "Maybe not, Colcord. Ben will cool off. Did you ever have a run-in with him before?" he queried curiously.

"Nothin' to speak of." Crip shrugged. "He likes to give orders," he allowed. "But up to now I've advised him to stay on his side of the line, and I'd do the same. Yuh believe me, don't yuh?" he broke off with some sharpness.

"If you say so." Pat saw no point in antagonizing him, and for that matter he was far from convinced that Colcord was the chief offender in the present case. "It happens I'm riding out your way, Crip. Were you on your way home by any chance?"

"Sure, I—" Colcord broke off. Grasping instinctively

at the stalwart support offered by this broad-shouldered, level-eyed man, the old fellow hesitated suspiciously. "Yuh wasn't figurin' on ridin' guard with me, Stevens?"

Pat laughed. "So far from it," he denied lightly, "that I was hoping to make free with your advice on the way. But you're too sharp for me. I might as well own up."

"Well, in that case—" Secretly gratified, Colcord tucked his belligerent chin in, looking modest. "Shall we get started?"

They mounted and jogged out of town in leisurely fashion. Not till Dutch Springs was some distance behind them did either venture to broach what was really on his mind.

"What was you wantin' to ask me about, boy?" Crip finally broke the ice.

Instead of answering directly, Pat turned the subject with adroit indirection. "What in the world do you suppose was old Cobb's object, Colcord?" he asked with a show of earnestness. "You swore you weren't after his grass, and I'll buy that. But he must have had something in mind."

Crip threw up his hands. "Who knows?" he exclaimed. "He caught me plumb off my guard, makin' a crazy charge I never even thought of. Since Marty got killed I'm inclined to think the old man is breakin' up, Stevens."

Pat pondered the matter. From the reply to his question it appeared that Colcord did not yet connect the occurrence in town with any deep-laid plot. "Has anything else come up between you two lately?" he pressed. "Have you had any trouble at all out there on Saw Buck?"

"Trouble?" Colcord looked at him oddly. "Like what, Stevens? Why should I have any trouble?"

"Last time it was beef stealing," was the level reply. "Cobb lost quite a few head that way—and it stands to reason you must have too."

"No, strange as it sounds, I didn't. I always took it for granted that stuff cropped up along with his trouble with Pack Traver," reminded Crip simply. "It stopped altogether at the time Traver was killed. And there hasn't been anything else to worry about. This range is pretty free of rustlin' just now." He shook his grizzled head. "You're barkin' up the wrong tree, Stevens."

"What about War Ax?" Pat persisted. "Does Stober ever give you any headaches?"

The creases at the corners of Colcord's faded eyes slowly deepened into an expression of caution. "No," he said briefly. "O' course his punchers come botherin' around Penny now and then. But that's all."

"Did you ever see anything queer going on over that way? Anything at all?"

"Look, Stevens." Old Crip spoke with nervous force. "War Ax is a big outfit—almost as big as I was once. I got my little spread out there, and a handful of cows. I try to pay attention to my own affairs. Don't get me involved in anything with my neighbors, will yuh? That's exactly what I'm tryin' to avoid with Cobb." It was a curious cross between a plea and a command.

"Oh, now." Pat was serene. "It seems to me that Cobb has already managed that—"

"He better unmanage it! He'll never prove his grass is half as good as what I already got. Let him do his damnedest! . . . What I'm afraid of, boy," Colcord pursued more temperately, "is that he'll try to take his meanness out on Kip McKinley. The old fellow never hurt nobody—and if Cobb has the gall to start any dirty work, he'll answer for it!"

"I don't believe he'll do that," Pat deprecated. "Unless he's scared into it."

Colcord looked at him carefully. "Scared? That old bobcat?" He barked an incredulous laugh. "What in the world do yuh mean by that?"

If Pat had some thought in mind that prompted the remark, he kept it to himself. Shaking his head instead, he turned the subject to old Crip's range as they drew near its borders.

Colcord was justly proud of Saw Buck. With a very few others now remaining, he had pioneered this country in his young days. Time was when he had held undisputed sway over half of Powder County. Easygoing and a bit reckless of chance, he had not had good luck in his later years. With no son to follow in his footsteps, he had sold off acreage until his ranch was one of the smallest.

Shrewd as ever, he had chosen well the land which he determined to hang onto. It was no exaggeration to say that Saw Buck comprised the best range in this end of Powder Valley. A clear stream tumbled out of the canyon behind his ranch, and the mountain blue stem was tall and lush.

"Yes—a nice little spread," Crip conceded modestly, glancing about the peaceful scene. "I made a mistake though, lettin' these other fellers ever crowd in on me. Why, I sold Chuck Stober his first chunk of land when he was glad to get a two-bit start!"

If Pat wondered why Stober should be mentioned in this connection he did not pursue it further. "I suppose you'll give McKinley orders to keep Saw Buck beef well back from Cobb's line—"

"I'll do nothin' of the kind!" Colcord exploded crisply. "He's always had them orders, Stevens. I don't doubt he's carried 'em out, no matter what that crazy Ben says!"

Penny Colcord was as good a puncher as any man. She was out on the range today and, seeing them coming across the swells, lost no time in riding forward. "How are you, Mr. Stevens?" She flashed a warm smile, remembering how he had quietly come to her support in Ganado.

"Hello, Penny." Pat beamed at her approvingly. "I see you're hard at it as usual—"

"Yes. So much must be done." She glanced across at her parent, her keen eye quick to pick up the signs of troubled concern in his face. "What is it, Dad? Did something happen there in town?" she asked swiftly.

"I'll say!" Colcord found himself impulsively blurting out the tale of Ben Cobb's sudden assault. Sobering, the girl heard him out with a frown. Pat guessed she did not welcome the news that Russ Cobb's father was leveling grave charges against them.

"Was Mr. Cobb serious?" she asked anxiously.

"Serious! That old jackass tried to take a shot at me!" Crip flared savagely, growing more heated as he thought about it. "He was so dang sure of himself! Do *you* know anything about our stock driftin' over onto Antler, girl?" he rasped.

Penny hesitated. Though by no means as ready to fly off the handle as Colcord himself, she was bothered. "As a matter of fact, Kip did say he had to drift a dozen or so head of our stuff back off of Antler range yesterday," she admitted.

"What—!" Colcord stared at her, affronted. "That don't make sense! What would persuade our fat Saw Buck cows to traipse over there?" He was aghast and unbelieving.

She spread her hands. "I talked it over with Kip," she acknowledged. "We agreed they *might* have been stampeded over there by a wolf or a cougar. But there was no fresh kill anywhere around—"

"Chased over there, yuh say?" Crip broke in harshly. "More likely by some dog in saddle leather, I'll warrant!"

Her delay was longer this time. "Kip swore as much himself," she confessed finally. "After we—found what I thought were fresh pony tracks. I wouldn't argue with him."

"Ain't no arguin' with plain common sense," Colcord averred stoutly. "Where is Kip? I want a talk with him—"

"He was over toward the canyon half an hour ago," she replied. "We ran the herd over toward the hills where it would be easier to keep an eye on it."

"Good enough. . . . And Daughter!" The old rawhide started away with a rush, only to halt. "Hereafter I don't want yuh to have no truck with them Cobbs, father or son. Yuh hear me?"

"Yes, Dad." It was barely audible, but apparently her word satisfied Crip. He barged off without a thought for Pat, who was satisfied to be left with Penny.

"Mr. Stevens, what is all this about, please?" she asked after a pause.

"Old Cobb jumped your father there in town about stealing his grass," replied Pat simply. "It sounded pretty much as if Ben really had a bug in his ear. . . . But you ought to be able to find out what's behind that," he broke off shrewdly.

"I—?" She looked surprised, and then turned pink. "I'm afraid I—don't see very much of Russ since he's been working for Mr. Stober, if that's what you mean," she explained hurriedly.

"That so?" He sounded scarcely convinced. "If you should see him, though, tackle him about what's eating his old man, eh?"

"Of course I shall." She spoke with resolution. "Any charge as serious as this cannot be ignored. Of course I don't know whether Russ will agree to discuss it with me," she added uncertainly.

"Try anyhow," urged Pat. "And if I see him, I will." He lifted his reins. "I won't need to remind you to keep an eye on your fire-eating dad for a few days, Penny? I'd say he ought to stick reasonably near the ranch—"

"I know." Penny said no more, but her expression spoke volumes. Pat was content to leave it at that. More levelheaded than Colcord, she had grasped the veiled threat to Saw Buck no less surely than he. And it was likely that she would control her headstrong parent with a hand steadier than his.

Turning away, Stevens concluded that no time was to be lost if he was to head off looming trouble before it became disaster. Making straight for the War Ax, he pushed along at a brisk pace until he reached the edge of Stober's range. Previous experience had taught him to use circumspection here. It could not warn him off altogether. A brief inspection told him that Russ Cobb's crew was not working at the old T Square today. No one at all was about the place.

Thrusting on, he began to cruise War Ax itself. More than once he was forced to draw back to avoid a meeting with working punchers. On one occasion he made sure he had been discovered, only to ride out of it by turning his back and jogging away as if he had every right on this range.

At the end of an hour's search he began to despair of locating young Cobb. Quite possibly the other was busy at the main ranch. Pushing on another mile, Pat had his perfunctory look at the east range. He was about to turn away when he halted abruptly to shade his eyes and stare steadily through the sun shimmer. A second later he grunted in relief.

Russ Cobb, working doggedly and alone on this far fringe of War Ax, was jarred out of an abstraction of his own to look up and find a swiftly advancing rider bearing down on him. Pat didn't give him time for speculation. "Look alive, Cobb," he called urgently. "Penny Colcord's in real trouble, and she can use some help!"

Russ stared rigidly for a bare instant. Recalling a previous meeting in Ganado, he could not doubt that Stevens came straight from the girl herself. Without further delay he yanked his bronc's head around and tore off across the range in the direction of Saw Buck.

[8]

Penny Colcord was as handy around the ranch as a man. Had she been left in sole charge of Saw Buck, she would have made as efficient a manager as her father. She knew cows and understood how to handle them. Old Crip was proud of her, seldom finding himself obliged to question her judgment. Kip McKinley took orders from her without question; and when, as on the present occasion, she found herself alone, she was accustomed to proceed with decision.

Finding more than a hundred head of Saw Buck steers gathered about a rocky water hole in a corner of the lower range, the girl put her wits to work. The graze hereabouts was not of the best. Yet she knew that unless something was done about it the stock would linger close to the water for hours.

Over in the direction of War Ax the grass was much richer. Due to Colcord's wary suspicions of the big rancher, he had ordered that the stock be kept off that part of the range. To Penny, however, this smacked of intimidation.

"I'll push the cows over that way and watch them myself," she decided. "Mr. Stober might as well steal our range outright as to keep us from using it ourselves."

It was not difficult for her to get the animals started in that direction and push them along. A critical glance at their gaunted flanks fully justified her course of action. Once satisfied that all was going well, she relaxed, allowing her thoughts to return to her talk with Pat Stevens. While clearly he meant well, she did not have much hope of his ability to influence Russ Cobb.

Once her warm friend, Russ had changed much since the disastrous feud with Pack Traver. She was obliged to admit the experience had suddenly made him a man, where before Russ had been a thoughtless boy. It was not all gain; the loss of his brother Marty seeming to have warned him to trust no one. That fatal clash with the T Square owner, moreover, seemed to have hardened Russ, making him act like another person, almost a stranger. Penny sighed unconsciously. Losing his friendship so abruptly, through no fault of her own, made her realize how much she had grown to depend on him.

Jarred out of her abstraction by the demands of her work, she spent some minutes in turning a stray or two in the right direction. Guarding the stock was second nature to her, and the stock recognized her authority.

Although no fence had ever been thrown up on this part of the range, Penny was entirely familiar with the limits of Saw Buck. Colcord's land still had another quarter of a mile to go in this direction when the girl began to check the steers on thick grass, allowing them to graze. She kept a strict watch as they began to spread out, making sure that none found the opportunity to slip out of sight in the clumps of brush.

At the same time she swept the surrounding range with watchful glance, on the lookout for strange riders. Thus it was that she first glimpsed a low smudge of what looked like dust some distance off to the south. For a few moments she gazed that way fixedly, attempting to determine its meaning.

"Whatever it is, it's over on War Ax," she thought with relief. "Perhaps Stober's men are moving some War Ax cattle—"

But as the seconds passed she suddenly realized that the dust pall was rolling this way at a rapid rate, and that it was growing in size. Alarm knifed through her now. "It *can't* be a range fire. I'd have smelled it—and the brush isn't dry enough! No stockman would be stupid enough to push a herd that fast. . . . It must be a stampede!"

The dust cloud, rising in angry billows now, was moving this way as surely as though aimed. Penny's heart sank with dread of what it might mean. Her fears had no power to panic her. Her first thought was for the Saw Buck stock. Hopeless as it looked, she set herself to the task of throwing her father's steers together and driving them out of the way.

To her exasperation the animals sensed some impending event. Growing nervous and scary, they proved all but impossible to control. If she sought to drive them one way they scattered and ran another, tossing their horns and rolling their eyes. An uneasy moaning and lowing set up. But Penny would not surrender. Working feverishly without visible result, she spared a desperate glance to the south.

The gray pall was advancing this way with what seemed the speed of a tornado, its baleful convolutions menacing. Barely a moment later she glimpsed the low, galloping wall of steers racing in the forefront. Wild-eyed and intent, in the grip of a nameless terror, they thundered on. The girl's breath sucked in sharply, dismay knifing her deep.

"I'll never make it," she gasped. "It'll be a miracle if I can save myself!"

Even now her wits had not ceased to work. Abandoning any real hope of saving the little Saw Buck herd in the face of that oncoming avalanche, she drew swiftly on her intimate knowledge of this range in the effort to save her own life. At no great distance was an outcrop ledge, thrust up like a knife-blade above the rolling range. Precarious as the shelter might be behind this dubious barrier, no other cover offered itself for a mile or more in any direction. The girl well knew how hopeless was any attempt to ride before the stampede, working gradually out of its way. In their madness that flood of steers might even overtake a horse and trample it down. It had to be the ledge, her common sense told her, or nothing.

Wheeling her trembling pony, she struck out for the ledge on a dead run. The stampede was sweeping close now, the hoofs of the racing steers a continuous, rumbling thunder. Guiding her terrified mount, she dared not spare a glance behind her. For several heartbreaking minutes it was a tossup whether she would ever reach the ledge at all.

It loomed close. Skirting its ragged end, the fleeting thought visited her that it was wholly inadequate as protection against such an avalanche of destruction. Once in its lee, it was all she could do to prevent the terror-stricken bronc from dashing straight on. Somehow she managed to haul it down to an uneasy stop, stamping and squealing in fright.

She had made it barely in time. Almost suffocated by the sense of hovering doom, she could only wait. Already the luckless Saw Buck stock was beginning to scatter and run. Next instant the stampede struck, its advancing wave sweeping by with a thunderous rush.

As Penny calculated, the runaway steers surged against the rocky ledge and parted, streaming by on either side. Some brushed by so close to her that she feared her pony might be knocked off its legs. Thick, hot dust rolled in, blinding and gritty. The air shook with the thunder of pounding hoofs. She could detect the trembling of the ground. For a brief space pandemonium enveloped her.

It seemed an endless time before that thundering terror slackened in the slightest. Her lungs labored. She had pulled her neckerchief up over her face to the eyes. It was poor protection in an atmosphere thicker than that of a dust storm. In the midst of it all she was forced to fight her pony sternly to prevent the animal from giving away to blind terror and carrying her into the midst of this tossing sea of charging, bellowing steers. How she managed it she could never have told.

Gradually, amost unbelievably, the nerve-jarring rumble and thunder lessened. Through eyes streaming with tears she could distinguish gaps in the flood of steers still lumbering by in slowly diminishing numbers. Her chest seemed about to burst, the heavy oppression gradually subsided as the dust pall slowly thinned to a gray fog.

"Thank goodness I'm still here," she thought tremulously. "But what will Dad say about our stock?"

That the little bunch of Saw Buck cattle had been swept away in the stampede she did not pause to question. What could have caused it? It had come with such terrifying suddenness that she had had no chance to question its origin or to attempt to read brands, even had she been able to. It was still all she could do to see her hand before her face.

Ten minutes later the lethal pall began noticeably to thin. Once certain of survival the girl had slipped to the ground, half-staggering as she leaned against her still quaking pony for support. Her senses threatened to desert her. She fought off the faintness she knew to be the result of nervous reaction.

"What can I do?" For once her thoroughly scattered wits seemed reluctant to function at all. "I must look for any of our beef there may be left—"

Despite her stoic courage, the tears continued to well up, streaking her dust-smeared cheeks. She knew well how little her father could afford the loss of even a per-

centage of his modest herd. This unwarned catastrophe
might easily be the equivalent of ruin.

"I'll have to tell him why I drove the stock out here,
into the path of that stampede," she reflected miserably.
"If only I hadn't been so conscientious—!"

A breeze was blowing today, which slowly dissipated
the lingering dust pall. At length she found herself able
to gaze about over what seemed a scene of desolation.
Brush had been knocked down and uprooted. The grass
had been chopped and ground into the dirt by hoofs
sharp as knives. Penny shuddered at the thought of what
she had barely escaped. Of the stampede itself there was
no longer any trace in sight. The terror-filled thunder was
gone utterly, and in its place had returned an ominous
silence.

Remounting with dragging limbs, she forced herself to
a practical consideration of any possible salvage—though
the prospect seemed dim indeed. She rode disconsolately
about the suddenly empty and soundless range, her eyes
filled with tears of grief and dismay. At length she spied
a limping steer, one of their own. In some miraculous
manner it had weathered the storm, remaining on its feet
after the stampede had passed. Refusing to allow herself
a ray of hope, the girl looked farther. In the course of
twenty minutes she was able to comb three or four sur-
viving steers out of the brush. But this seemed only an
ironical remnant after the loss of so many.

Minutes later a faint cry reached her ears. Penny
scarcely noticed. When Russ Cobb raced forward, hauling in a yard or two away, she looked at him dazedly.

"Penny! You here? What's this all about?" he ripped
out hoarsely. "What happened here anyway?"

She made a hopeless gesture. "You see. One moment
I was guarding Father's stock, and the next—this."

"I spotted all the signs of a run over here," he got out
swiftly. "You can't mean you were caught in it—?" He
stared at her disheveled appearance with cold horror.

"I'm—afraid I was." It was all she could manage at
the moment.

He shook his head in a puzzled way. "Stevens said you were in trouble. I never guessed it was this bad!"

That jarred her. "How could he have known?" she exclaimed wonderingly. "It came so suddenly!"

Cobb found no time to discuss the enigma. "What did happen, Penny?"

In a spate of words she told of drifting a part of her father's herd to better grass, concluding with the unforeseen and disastrous result. The Saw Buck stock was gone, swept away so completely as to have never been. Russ sobered, frowning as he listened.

"We can't let this pass," he exclaimed tightly. "It's not your dad I'm worried about—but what will such a loss do to you?"

She seemed not to have heard. "What will it do to Father?" she burst out apprehensively. "It will kill him—"

He shook a dogged denial. "Not if I can help it, girl."

His promise of aid appeared scarcely to reach her intelligence. "It's too late! What *can* be done?" she countered forlornly.

"Plenty," he caught her up. "A stampede can't run forever. I can't imagine where this one came from—except a passing trail herd. But I can find out. Your pa's stuff is bound to be with it!"

She shook her head hopelessly. "It would be fine of you to try. But I—can't honestly expect anything, Russ."

Cobb refused to listen. "I'm wasting time here, Penny! But you'll hear from me, one way or another. Try and keep up your spunk." He whirled his bronc as he spoke, starting away with a bound.

For several seconds she gazed after him through still misty eyes. Then as if suddenly awakened, she threw up her arm impulsively. "Goodbye, Russ! Be careful!" she called clearly, putting into her voice all the mingled hope and dread she felt.

Cobb waved back briefly, scarcely bothering to look back. All his keen faculties were bent on the problem in hand. It was a question how long this self-imposed task would take. Beyond a doubt his employer would have things to say about his absence. Russ did not care in the least; nor did he take time to marvel over the strong impulse which was carrying him away from his own interests. Penny Colcord was in trouble. That was enough for him to know.

There was no difficulty about following the course of the mad stampede. It had ripped a path across Saw Buck that would have been plain to a child. So intent was Russ on his purpose that, riding swiftly in the wake of the runaway stock, he did not miss the slightest indication of its progress.

His first discovery was disturbing. Less than a mile from where he had found the girl he came across the clear prints of a shod cow pony. A brief search turned up others, and Russ knew for certain that men had accompanied the stampede. It was not strange that Penny had seen nothing of them. The wonder was that she had survived at all. Only a long training in the meeting of range emergencies had saved her.

For Cobb the evidence presented other problems. Who were the men with the runaway herd, and how would he deal with them? At first glance it might seem that he could reasonably expect any assistance needed. But a close acquaintance with working punchers warned him otherwise. These men would be worn out and on edge; they might refuse to listen to him at all. The thought failed to slacken his pace.

The knowledge that he would have hard-boiled drovers to deal with was followed presently by a further shock. In a straggling wash that had been in the path of the stampede he spotted the prone form of a steer. Not yet dead, the animal began to struggle weakly when he drew close. Russ saw at once what had happened.

Knocked off balance in the sweeping avalanche of the stampede, the steer had suffered a broken leg. It was trampled and battered, obviously done for. But what jolted Cobb was the unmistakable War Ax brand burned on its dusty flank.

"War Ax!" he blurted, at a loss. "Why I never knew Stober was driving a trail herd today—"

He delayed long enough to put the steer out of its misery with a single shot. Then urging his bronc out of the wash, he rode on at top speed after the racing stampede.

It was nearly an hour before the dust haze raised by the racing stock took form in a rolling pall several miles ahead. Watching keenly, Russ decided that it was moving more slowly. Pressing on, he never let up until, topping a long swell overlooking the barren desert hollow below, he saw that the stampede was at last under control. Still widely scattered, the stock was allowing itself to be bunched and held.

Though he stopped a few busy riders with sweat-stained shirts and dust-caked faces, Russ got little attention from any of them, grimly intent on their work as they were. Dropping down off the swell and making for a rider who appeared to be calling out orders, he steeled himself for argument. It was no longer a surprise to him, a few moments later, to learn that the man was Bat Doyle, one of Chuck Stober's brassy foremen. Clearly Doyle was acting today as trail boss. Oddly enough, Russ detected in his bluff demeanor no trace of exasperation over the stampede.

"What came off here, Bat?" he called as he drew near.

Doyle greeted his appearance stolidly. "Little run," he disposed of the event briefly. "No great harm done, I don't reckon."

"No harm done!" Cobb stared at him. "Don't you know you busted clean through Crip Colcord's range with this cyclone—and that over a hundred head of Saw Buck stuff is mixed in with ours?"

"So what?" Doyle shrugged. "His loss ain't mine."

"But aren't you planning to cut Colcord's stuff out and turn it back?" demanded Russ incredulously.

"You crazy, kid?" Bat gave a coarse laugh. "I should work for Colcord! It's his fault for gettin' in our way. He'll have to like it, buddy. Because it's happened now!"

[9]

Russ Cobb stared at the burly trail boss for a long moment in frank disbelief. He was fully aware that many War Ax employees were not notorious for their fairness and honesty; but this was beyond the bounds of common reason.

"Man, you can't hope to get away with it," he protested vehemently. "It amounts to ruin for Colcord! Even Stober himself will be on your neck about it!"

Doyle was not impressed by the argument. "Look," he said cynically, "I'm makin' a delivery. As it happens I've got a famous start. Is it your idea that I'll spend a whole day cuttin' a handful of cows out of this herd to please you or anybody else?" His laugh this time was sarcastic. "Come again, Cobb! Tell Stober to credit old Colcord with twenty head, if yuh want to. I got no time to fool around."

Red with indignation, Russ tried to argue. But Doyle gave him no opportunity, turning his horse away as he called gruff orders to his men. Russ gazed about him with the exasperation of hopeless rage. He was powerless and he knew it.

Bunching the stock, the War Ax crew proceeded to get it moving again as matter-of-factly as if nothing out of the ordinary had happened. Finding it impossible to rectify the outrageous situation, young Cobb followed doggedly for a time. He accosted a puncher or two, calling attention angrily to Bat Doyle's brazen tactics.

The men gave him small sympathy. After several ineffectual attempts, the big trail boss himself deigned to grant Russ his hard attention once more, turning sharply back.

"Look, buster," he bellowed at Cobb, "I know yuh work for Stober. Yuh don't belong in my crew, and I don't see yuh helpin' here. So trot along, before I start chargin' you board!"

Though by no means intimidated, Russ saw clearly enough that he would get nowhere with this craggy hard shell. He turned back, scowling in sheer chagrin. What would he tell Penny Colcord now, after promising her aid?

Backtracking the way he had come, he made straight for Saw Buck, though he was no longer in a hurry. His embittered thoughts dwelled on the situation as he saw it, and for the first time he understood thoroughly that Penny's father shared the lot of all small ranchers at the hands of men like Stober.

"It's just an accident that that stampede hit Colcord, instead of Dad," he reflected soberly. "Stober wouldn't make any distinction between the two. Maybe I'm a fool to be working for War Ax—but at least I can keep an eye on things."

It was late afternoon by the time he reached the spot where he had left the girl. She was nowhere in sight; yet he made sure of this before shoving on toward the Colcord ranch. As he neared the place his pace grew even slower than before. It was with the greatest reluctance that he forced himself directly to the ranch house in search of the girl.

Seeing his approach from the house, Penny stepped out into the yard. Hope faded from her anxious eyes as she perceived his lack of haste and downcast expression. "You're back, Russ," she greeted him, with a weak attempt at a smile. "You—had no luck?"

"I know what happened, if that's what yuh mean." Dismounting slowly, young Cobb avoided her eye, half-ashamed of what he must say and putting it off from second to second.

"We knew that before," she reminded him gently.

"No, Penny." His headshake was stubbornly honest, however hard he found it to thrust on. "I've got to tell you it was a War Ax herd that ripped through here and carried your dad's stuff away—"

She held her breath, gazing at him fixedly. *"You* are

telling me that, Russ?" she got out wonderingly. *"You* —caught up with them, then? Are . . . they turning Dad's cattle back?" she managed to frame the vital question.

"No. I demanded that the stuff be cut out, Penny," he drove on miserably. "And Bat Doyle refused. He— laughed at the idea!"

She gasped. "You can't mean—" Penny broke off, hot indignation flaming in her cheeks. "Surely it can't be possible that War Ax intends to sweep up our stock so casually, and keep it?"

Desperation crept into his worried eyes. "Penny, you've got to understand! I work for War Ax, I know; but I've got no authority over there. I'm not even supposed to know about this drive!" He was pleading now, aware of her growing coldness of manner. "Stober will straighten this out when he hears about it. I'm sure of it!"

The girl gave him scant encouragement. "I'm sure we wouldn't care to depend on his—generosity," she retorted tartly. "Is there a reason why we must?"

"But you don't get it! It's not Stober who's doing this to your dad. It's that bullheaded Doyle who wouldn't listen to reason! Stober will call him to order quick enough the minute he learns about this—"

"Father desires no favors," Penny stated with icy finality. "I'm quite sure I feel the same. We ask only to be left alone by Mr. Stober and all his help!"

Her manner of putting it cut off any hopes Cobb had that she would understand his position. Refusing to admit defeat, he was still arguing against hopeless odds when the clatter of pony hoofs broke through his protestations of innocence, and two men rode around the corner of the house. Penny's father was in the lead, and Pat Stevens was with him. Drawing rein, old Crip glared at the young fellow severely.

"War Ax hand, ain't you?" he brought out with stern hostility. "What are yuh doin' here, boy?"

Russ fought his flaring temper and mastered it. "Mr.

Colcord, I've been trying to help you. Something happened to your cattle—"

"I know all about it," Crip interrupted forbiddingly. "I know the part War Ax had in it too. I'm plumb surprised you've got the gall to show your face here!"

Cobb's brows shot up in astonishment. "Hold that, Colcord." His voice hardened. "I didn't even know anything was going on over here! Stevens tipped me off— he'll tell you so himself." He paused, shooting a look at Pat. "How *did* you know so much, anyhow?"

"I didn't, Cobb." Pat's unbroken calm was exasperating. "I sent you over here, hoping you could straighten things out with Penny," he acknowledged simply. "Colcord and I found out what happened later. I'll grant from personal knowledge that you had nothing whatever to do with it," he added.

"That's easy said." Old Crip was dogmatic. "Ben Cobb tried t' knock me down there in Dutch Springs! Accused me of stealin' his grass—" He snorted. "And what's more, Cobb, he swore you was watchin' me and seen it!" He made a violent gesture. "I'll grant it's naural for you to play your old man's game—but don't expect me to be taken in. Why lie about it? I don't trust none of your breed as far as I can see yuh!"

Russ went red and then white. "If Dad said that—" he began, and choked. When he resumed again the words came slowly. "It's simply not true that I've been watching you, or Kip McKinley for that matter, or that I accused you of anything," he declared flatly. "Dad's old, Colcord, and apt to be cantankerous. It could be he's been listening to gossip and was striking back blindly—I don't know."

"If you don't know, who does?" With the vindictiveness of the injured party, Crip pressed his advantage brutally. "I think yuh do, all right. And furthermore, mister, I'm satisfied that you and your worthless father are workin' together against me!"

Desperation flickered in Cobb's tight face. Seeing his hopes of reconciliation with the girl shattered, he still attempted to control his leaping anger.

"I'll be waiting for the day when you're forced to swallow those words, Colcord," he cried. "What could I hope to gain from ruining you? As for my workin' for War Ax, Stober would fire me if he knew I was over here talkin' to you right now!"

"If you go back where you belong, you won't be caught talkin' to me," retorted Crip fiercely. "I can stand it—so what are you waitin' for?"

Staring at them one after another, Russ found no encouragement whatever. Penny was obviously waiting for him to leave, her face closed. Pat's expression could not be read. But he did not offer to intercede.

Russ shook his head. "You're dead wrong about me," he averred. "Someday I'll prove that to you. I can't now." Turning, he swung astride and rode out of the ranch yard in an unbroken silence.

Old Crip waited till he was gone, then snorted softly. "Good riddance," he growled. Penny looked at him queerly. Without a word then, she turned on her heel and ran to the house, entering at the door without a backward glance. Colcord ignored her departure.

"What'll I do now, Stevens?" he demanded. "I can't let Stober get away with this kind of barefaced rustlin'!"

Pat appeared undisturbed. "Oh, I expect he'll square it, as Cobb says," he stated quietly. "Do you want me to see what I can do about it, Colcord?"

"Go ahead." Though privately dubious about the results, Crip looked grateful for the offer.

"Understand, though," reminded Pat strictly. "If I do anything at all about this, I want it left entirely in my hands. No squabbling with Ben Cobb, or anything like that. Is it a deal?"

Crip nodded, swallowing his bitter grudge with difficulty. "I'll consider my hands tied till yuh either get that stock back, or don't," he agreed. "After that I'm claimin' the right to act as I think best."

"The beef is gone, of course," Pat pointed out. "But it's common practice for a man to settle up for other brands that turn up in his drive. Stober undoubtedly sold for a high enough figure to clear you a profit. I'll keep that in mind."

They talked for a few minutes longer, but it was clear that, with this new mission in hand, Stevens was impatient to get away. He left presently, promising to keep Colcord posted on developments.

Leaving Saw Buck, Pat had no thought of proceeding at once to War Ax. Dusk was closing in as he rode into Dutch Springs. Eating supper in the restaurant, he lounged about the Gold Eagle for an hour, talking with friends, before turning abruptly to Jess Lawlor and tapping him on the arm.

"I want a word with you, Jess," he announced.

Grunting, the lawman followed him to the street without a question. Once beyond earshot of interested townsmen, Pat halted to face his companion. Without preamble he plunged into a narrative of events on Colcord's Saw Buck.

"Stober's got a sizable bunch of Crip's cows in that drive of his," he ended, making it plain that he spoke from personal observation. "I don't anticipate any great difficulty in seeing that he pays for them. But the thing is, Jess, that he may make a big fuss about its being an act of God—and after he bought out Pack Traver as he did," he pointed out shrewdly, "we're at least able to guess different! It'll simplify matters if you're along when I go out there and talk to him."

"Since it's an open and shut case," demurred Lawlor gruffly, "I can't see why yuh need me—"

"You heard the man warn me to stay away from War Ax," reminded Pat crisply. "Lord knows why—but there it is. This time he might not wait to see if I'm out there on business or not."

"Well, since yuh put it that way." Seeing no way out of the onerous chore, Lawlor knit his rugged brows. "Tomorrow'll have to do then, Stevens. I can't get away like this at the drop of a hat."

Pat ignored his poorly hidden irritation, nodding readily. "Can't go myself before then," he seconded. "I'll pick you up in the morning."

Lawlor seemed to have worked himself into a better frame of mind by the following day. Pat met him at his office after breakfast and they shoved off at once. It was no accident that, leaving the beaten trails, Pat led the way across the range, skirting Saw Buck, so that the sheriff could see with his own eyes the evidences of the stampede. Lawlor looked around sharply, but said nothing.

They thrust on, presently reaching War Ax's boundary. Stevens still maintained silence, letting Jess think his own thoughts. If his expression meant anything, Lawlor was primed for an argument by the time they drew up at Stober's ranch.

The place was as usual a bustle of activity. No one appeared to pay any attention whatever to their arrival. Lawlor's roar quickly brought a ranch hand running. On their inquiry for the War Ax owner, the first report was that Stober was not at home. Not to be shrugged off so easily, Jess only nodded.

"We can wait. Eat good here, don't yuh?"

Whether or not his firmness put a different face on things, a short time thereafter Stober himself put in an appearance. He affected surprise at seeing them.

"Howdy, Sheriff!" He looked about frowning. "Why wasn't I told you were here—?"

The lame excuse for delay rated no credit whatever with his visitors. Passing it over in silence, Lawlor turned straight to business. "I expect yuh know your herd stampeded yesterday, Stober—"

"I did hear something about it." Chuck's stony eyes slitted. "No great harm done, I understand," he added quickly.

"To you—no," seconded Jess, speaking with dry particularity. "But that run of yours picked up a bunch of Saw Buck stock, in case yuh didn't hear about that—and Colcord's naturally pretty concerned about it."

"Oh?" Stober put on a sceptical air. "You could've been misinformed about that, of course. These little ranchers are always screaming foul. I'm sure Doyle would cut out any beef he picked up purely by accident—"

"He didn't though." Lawlor was dogged. "That very

point came up, Stober, if yuh need to be told. Your man Doyle refused to do anything of the kind."

The War Ax owner regarded him coolly. "Just who told you that?" he countered in a grating tone.

"No matter." Jess waved the point aside authoritatively. "I'm takin' it as proved. So I reckon you'll have to."

Stober shrugged. "Oh well. That can be settled as soon as Doyle gets back. I'll tend to it right off and let you know," he promised easily.

Lawlor's neck began to swell and his jaws bulged ominously. "Get this, mister. I'm here to represent the law—and I'm askin' you to settle this now."

"Oh, if you insist, of course!" Chuck put on a tolerant air, managing to suggest by his manner that he considered it petty tactics on Lawlor's part. "But Colcord can hardly expect to collect before *I* get paid," he proceeded blandly.

"Yes he can." Pat spoke up before the lawman could fall a prey to this specious reasoning. "Old Crip doesn't have your resources to fall back on, Stober. He never expected to be hit by a stampede your men plainly should have prevented. And I'm sure he never asked you to market his stock for him." He shook his head. "This is a case where you're criminally liable—not that anyone would look at it that way as long as you square right up."

Stober regarded him wickedly, then turned to Jess. "Is this—range lawyer speaking for you?" he demanded challengingly.

"He's speakin' for Crip Colcord," Lawlor tossed back. "Is there a difference?"

Clearly the last thing Stober wanted was any real appearance of flouting the law. Carefully manipulated, it had always been his bulwark and mainstay. His shrug was a masterpiece of resignation. "Naturally I don't want to be considered unfair," he allowed. "How many head does Colcord claim to have lost?"

Jess looked at Stevens expectantly. Pat was ready for the question. "The figure was well over two hundred," he said evenly, naming a preposterously generous number. "I'll undertake to persuade Crip to settle for that. And you can check with Doyle—when he gets back," he added, knowing he was turning the knife in the other man.

Naked hatred smoldered in Stober's beady eyes. But he knew better than to haggle about it now. "Well . . . all right. I'll see that he gets a check to cover," he said gruffly.

Impatient of his stalling, Lawlor shook his head decisively. "I'm figurin' to lay that check in Colcord's hand myself," he announced stolidly.

Defeated and fully aware of it, Stober delayed a bare second before throwing up a hand. "It's a nuisance, Lawlor, but if you'll wait I'll have to make it out, I suppose," he capitulated grudgingly, turning toward the house as if glad to get away from them.

He did make them wait but when Lawlor tucked the check in his pocket at last, showing no trace of impatience, he only winked slyly at Pat. "Thanks," he said sarcastically.

[10]

Stevens and the sheriff were barely beyond sight of War Ax before the former spoke up. "Jess, you told Stober you aimed to lay the check in Colcord's hand yourself," he began easily. "I expect that was only for argument's sake—"

"Why, I made up my mind I'd get that check one way or another." Lawlor's stiff smile faded as he glanced across. "You got something in mind, Stevens?"

Pat admitted as much. "It's just a thought," he amplified. "But you must've heard there's been a little friction between Crip and old Ben Cobb. . . . It struck me that if young Russ was to turn that check over to Colcord him-self, it might help to patch it up. I'd see to it that it got where it belongs, of course," he added.

The lawman rasped his jaw with a palm. "It ain't strictly accordin' to regulation, Stevens. But there might just be somethin' in that," he opined after a delay. "Heading off trouble is a whole lot cheaper than straight-enin' it out later. But can yuh make young Cobb see it that way?"

"I'll take it in hand, if you want," Pat offered. "It just happens that I know Russ is pretty anxious to make a hit with Colcord's girl. This would do it," he pointed out. "Leave it to Russ to see that quick enough."

Lawlor's brow cleared. "That's sense," he conceded. Fumbling in his pocket he found the folded check and handed it over. "There's times when I'm not so sure about you, mister. But you do use your noggin once in a while. I don't suppose you'd consider a deputy's badge—?"

It was an old point of discussion between them. Pat smiled. "Thanks, Jess. That's a compliment. But Lazy Mare keeps me pretty busy most of the time, as you know. If I change my mind for any reason I'll speak up."

They were well past Saw Buck on their way back to town before Lawlor reminded himself of Stober's check, now safely tucked in Pat's shirt pocket. "Are yuh headin' for Antler now, or what?" he asked.

Pat shrugged. "Russ is pretty hot right now." He told how Crip Colcord had virtually accused the puncher of engineering the stampede. "We'll let them simmer down a bit. I'll see him around."

"Well—" Jess was willing to leave it to his judgment. "Just don't let Colcord hang and rattle too long. From all I hear the old boy's primed for trouble."

But Pat thought otherwise. "I'd judge old Cobb to be the one who would bear watching," he returned. "I'd give something to know who's been at him, and what's going through his head right now."

As a matter of fact, Ben was asking himself what it was that made Russ hang around Antler so persistently today. Usually his son was up before daylight and off to his work at the Stober ranch. This morning Russ stayed at home and seemed to avoid his father, his manner preoccupied.

"Hey, boy," old Ben called out gruffly at length. "It's gettin' late for yuh to be stickin' around here. Ain't been fired over at War Ax, have yuh?"

Russ hesitated briefly, then shook his head. "Nothing like that," he denied hurriedly. "But work has gone a little slack right now—"

"On a big spread like Stober's?" Even Ben knew better than that. "Why, he don't never run out of work, and you know it!"

Russ made an impatient gesture. "To tell the truth," he confessed a little sharply, "I haven't made up my mind yet. But I'm thinking about quitting, Dad."

"Yuh are! What happened?" Ben stared at the young fellow steadily. "Don't tell me Stober gave yuh a dressin' down about somethin'—"

"No, no." Russ frowned. "The only thing he could say that would bother me is, 'You're fired.' He hasn't yet."

"What is it then?" probed Cobb, plainly mystified. "You ain't gettin' lazy all of a sudden? Because the money you're makin' has been a big help—and you're workin' for yourself, you know. Antler'll be yours someday."

Russ waved this aside. "It isn't anything like that at all, Pa," he protested.

"Then what is it?" Ben pinned him shrewdly to the answer.

Once started, Russ found himself blurting out the story of the stampede. "It slammed straight through Saw Buck—and putting two and two together, I'm satisfied that Stober must have wanted it that way," he wound up soberly.

To his surprise his father found nothing unwelcome in the announcement. "Ploughed right across Colcord's spread, did it? I reckon it tore up his range pretty bad—"

"Tore up the range? Why, it took a good share of Crip's herd with it!" Suppressed indignation made Russ vehement. "And when I overtook him, Bat Doyle flatly refused to cut the stuff out and turn it back!"

"Good for him!" Old Cobb appeared frankly delighted. "I wouldn't myself. . . . By gravy, it serves Crip right, the old reprobate! Must've hit him pretty hard, too. I hope it drives him plumb off the range!"

Russ could hardly believe his ears. "Dad! You can't mean that. Crip Colcord's our neighbor. If you have your differences with him, that's no reason for wishing him ruined!"

"Ain't, eh?" Ben gave a guttural chuckle. "Dang him, I'm fed to the teeth with his snide tricks, boy, and yuh might's well know it." He paused here, adding cynically, "But I know what's botherin' yuh. Yuh been moonin' over that girl of his till yuh can't see things straight no more!"

It was so near the fact, without being true at all, that Russ found the charge intolerable. "Cut it out, Dad," he cried harshly. "You know that's not so! Even if it was, Penny Colcord's got nothing to do with Crip's stealing our grass—which I never did see, and find no reason for anyhow!"

"Ain't, huh?" Ben stuck to the only point which he knew he could successfully argue. "She could see to it that Colcord got rid of that ornery Kip McKinley in ten minutes, if you passed her the word. But has she done it?" He snorted derisively. "That ought to tell plain enough whose side she's on—only you don't want to see it, boy."

Russ attempted to reason with him. "I told you you've got those Colcords dead wrong," he burst out. "And McKinley's an old man who needs a job. He's so far from looking for trouble that he'd go out of his way to avoid it—"

Cobb glowered at his son suspiciously. "Well, now. Been makin' love to you too, has he? Maybe it's about time I asked myself whose side *you're* on," he rasped sarcastically. "By grab, I thought I taught yuh better sense, boy—right after we seen what happened to Marty, too!"

Unable to make the slightest headway against such incorrigible hostility, Russ turned his back and flung away. Swinging into the saddle, he scarcely noted what direction he was taking. There was an injustice in his parent's stubborn wrong-headedness which left him wretched. Penny Colcord had never done anything in her life to harm Ben Cobb. But already his father's fanatic suspicions had robbed Russ of such sympathy as she may have felt for him.

It was utterly impossible to argue with Cobb. How to turn him from his disastrous course before the results of his folly rebounded on himself, Russ was at a total loss to discover. The young fellow liked Penny more than he had ever cared for any girl. That he must lose her seemed certain. He rebelled fiercely at the thought that any harm might come to either her or her father through a member of his own family.

Noting presently that he had blindly taken the trail to Dutch Springs, Russ thrust on. It mattered little where he went until he was done fighting the battle of his thoughts.

So preoccupied was he that he took it at first as an annoyance when someone hailed him as he rode slowly into town. Glancing around half-attentively, he recognized Pat Stevens with no more than languid interest.

"Over here, Russ—if you're not too busy." Pat gestured him forward good-humoredly. "I've been wanting a word with you."

Little enough inclined to submit to useless advice, young Cobb complied indolently. "No use, Stevens," he remarked as he dismounted. "I'm not in a listening mood right now—"

"You'll hear this though." Pat told how Sheriff Lawlor and himself had made a diplomatic visit to War Ax. "I though Stober would listen to the law quicker than he would to me. He did." Pat pulled out the check Lawlor had turned over to him, letting Cobb read its face. "Maybe you'd better take this out to Colcord before his heart breaks."

For an instant Russ hardly comprehended. Then his heart bounded. "Why, that's—it covers Colcord's loss in that stampede!" he exclaimed. "You're doing this for me, Stevens. . . . *Was it that much?*" His eyes searched Pat's face while he tried to interpret the other man's flickering smile. "I . . . see. You made the amount generous while you were about it—is that it?"

"I couldn't see any reason for underestimating." Pat's shrug said that Stober could afford it. "Shall we discuss it awhile, or had you ought to get yourself out there and relieve the old man's mind?"

Agitation seized Russ at the prospect of the interview with Crip Colcord which he saw looming. "He'll never believe this is on the level," he exclaimed.

"I don't suppose he will." Pat was unruffled. "But he'll take it. And there's Penny to think about—"

Russ's face hardened at mention of the girl's name. "What about her?" he grated.

"Why, she's an interested party." Pat looked innocent. "In your shoes, I wouldn't hesitate to do anything I could for her. Maybe she can persuade Crip to keep out of old Ben's hair till he cools off. You never know."

Grasping at any straw, young Cobb subsided. He took the check, turning it over a time or two; then deliberately tucking it away, he prepared to remount. "It sounds okay, Stevens." He was speaking under tight self-control. "I'll thank you later, when we see how this works out."

A smile tugging at his jaws, Pat watched him jog briskly out of town. Wholly unaware of the difference in his demeanor, Cobb lost no time heading straight for Saw Buck. He paid small heed when, an hour later, a grizzled old-timer rode hastily forward to intercept him as he pushed across Colcord's range toward the ranch.

"You again, Cobb? What you after here—?" It was Kip McKinley, aged and ineffectual, yet fiercely loyal to his employer's interests.

"Good news for old Crip, McKinley, if you want to know! Stober sent over a fat check to cover that lost beef." Waving the slip of paper airily, Russ thrust on while the wrinkled puncher gaped after him with sagging jaw.

Cobb saw the colored flutter of Penny's dress as he neared the ranch. A moment later, after gazing his way, the girl stepped into the house. It dampened Russ's enthusiasm to see again how she felt about him. But he was resolute.

"Crip Colcord. . . . Hey, Crip!" he called, easing his seat in the saddle while he waited in the yard.

It was several minutes before Colcord emerged, showing no haste. His manner cooled as he spotted Cobb. "What now?" he barked gruffly.

Dismounting, Russ noted out of the corner of his eye that Penny was watching from the door. Stepping forward, he extracted the check from his pocket and extended it. "This is yours," he announced stolidly.

Crip was at first contemptuous, then his eyes sharpened as he saw that it was a check. "Mine—?" He grabbed at it—and was silent for so long that Penny was drawn irresistibly out of the door.

"What is it, Dad?"

"It's a check, Daughter—with Stober's signature." Reading the figures, Colcord leaned forward for a better look. He was frankly perplexed. He began to tremble. "Why, hang it! Is this some rotten joke of his? It can't be for that stock of mine he stole—"

Enjoying this more than he had expected, Cobb only shrugged. "Don't it cover?" he grunted.

Crip let out an exclamation. "Why, it—it more than—" He halted that, rattling the check agitatedly. *"Is this good?"*

Penny had her look, her eyes widening. "Oh—Russ!" Gladness rang in her voice. "It will save us!" Before he guessed what she was about, she rushed close, throwing her arms about him and hugging him soundly. She stepped back then, her cheeks pink; there could no longer be any doubt of her full approval.

Striving to pretend he didn't notice, Russ found his voice. "I expect the check's all right," he got out as steadily as he could manage. "If I was you though, I'd get it to the bank fast, Colcord."

Crip nodded, half beside himself with joy at this unexpected good fortune. Far too rattled to question its source, he sought to think rationally. "I'll do that—"

"Do it right now," Russ urged. "I'll ride along with you to make sure everything's all right."

"This is white of yuh, boy." Barely able to think what to do first, Colcord rushed around, grabbing up his saddle and then dropping it to snake a bronc out of the corral. Equally excited for the moment, Penny helped him. After much fumbling the pony stood saddled and ready.

"Please be careful," the girl exclaimed as they prepared to start. "And Dad, if I don't hear from you at once I'll certainly follow!"

Cobb laughed, finding warm comfort in her words. "No harm in that, Penny. But I'll look after him," he assured.

"I know you will," she returned fervently. "And Russ —I don't know how I'll ever thank you for what you've done!"

It was Colcord himself who returned most quickly to his native caution on the ride to town. "This ain't one of Stober's tricks?" he demanded, looking at the check for the tenth time. "It simply ain't like him to be so generous!"

"What makes you think he's being generous?" demanded Russ. "If you haven't got it yet, he made out that check because he was told to."

"Well, I don't know." Colcord marveled stubbornly. "To be plain about it, boy—between Ben Cobb's son and that Stober, I just can't hardly believe it!"

At the slur on his father, merited though he knew it to be, Russ felt faint irritation. "All right, all right. Put that check away, will you, before you lose it?"

His private fear was lest they should run into a knot of War Ax hands, primed for just this situation. Moreover, it was natural to share a modicum of Colcord's own doubt of the check's authenticity. To Cobb's relief they reached Dutch Springs without anything happening. Yet he was concerned, on riding past the place, to note two ponies bearing the War Ax brand tethered at the rack before the Gold Eagle.

If Colcord had any remote idea of stopping elsewhere before going on to the bank, Russ disabused him. "Keep going," he urged. "Let's get this over with, Colcord, so you'll know exactly where you stand."

By no means reluctant, Crip made straight for the stone bank building, impressive of size and appearance for this modest cow town. They dismounted in front of the place in time to see Ab Keeler's cashier pulling the shades down inside.

"Oh, oh." His face grave, Russ hurried to the nearest window, tapped, and when he got the cashier's attention, motioned toward the door. To his disgust the man shook his head decidedly.

"Closin' up, are they? I reckon Ab'll let me in." Hiding the tremor of uneasiness in his voice, Colcord hobbled to the door and tried it. It was locked. Grasping the handle firmly, Crip rattled it as loudly as he could.

The cashier appeared inside, making violent motions. Colcord persisted. "Where's Keeler?" he bawled, red in the face. "Get him out here!"

It was some moments before the rotund banker himself, clad in shirtsleeves and with a pen behind his ear, put in an appearance. Peering near-sightedly through the glass, he made out who it was.

"Vault's locked, Colcord," his muffled voice came through to them. "We're closed for business—"

When Crip showed signs of an intention to rip the heavy door from its hinges, Keeler resignedly threw the bolts back. "What is it, men?" he demanded, opening up.

Colcord thrust out the check. "I want that cashed right now, Ab. And dont tell me yuh ain't got the money!"

Keeler looked at it for a space in silence. Shaking his head, he started to hand it back. "Sorry, Crip," he growled. "I got to tell you I couldn't honor this even if I was open for business—which I ain't!" His white mustache bristling, he started to thrust the big door shut once more.

[11]

"Hold on, Keeler." Russ Cobb thrust forward to hold the bank door open when the rotund banker tried to push it shut. "This is no ordinary occasion. Colcord has got a perfectly good check here. I know for a fact that Stober made it out to cover a legitimate debt. So cash it for the man, and let's not have any fancy talk!"

Old Ab gave him a pained look. "You just don't listen, boy," he retorted austerely. "I just got done sayin' I'm not authorized to cash this check. That'll have to be final."

Russ stared at him in astonishment. "What does that mean—final? This *is* a bank, isn't it? You can't mean that Stober hasn't an account here? Isn't his personal check good—?"

Keeler began to get his dander up. "I don't consider myself bound to answer your questions, young man! I told yuh what the situation is. Now go away. I've got my own work to do here—"

"But Ab, you don't savvy." Colcord attempted to use another form of persuasion. "A stampede of Stober's cattle picked up a bunch of my stuff, and Chuck is payin' for it. I can't stand such a loss—and with Stober's settlement I don't have to. That puts it squarely up to you, man. Why should you be tryin' to ruin me?"

It was the first word Keeler had heard of the stampede and its consequences. He sobered. "Sorry to hear of your trouble of course. But my instructions have nothing to do with your predicament, Colcord," he reminded strictly. "If yuh plan to borrow, come to me at a reasonable hour and I'll consider it."

"I don't want to borrow no money," Crip roared. "*You* be reasonable, and I won't have to! Hang it all—"

Cobb listened briefly to their haggling, and swiftly

91

decided that the overly cautious banker would not be open to persuasion. Had Stober already managed to stop payment on the check? Stevens had as much as admitted that it had literally been forced out of the man. Filled with disgust, Russ turned sharply on his heel, starting away.

An idea had come to him. When he had ridden in with Colcord he had taken keen note of the brands on the horses lining the hitch rails. Pat's pony had been among the rest. If he could get hold of the Lazy Mare owner and get him down here quickly enough, perhaps Stevens might be able to straighten the matter out. It was worth a try.

As it happened, Pat was standing with Sam Sloan in front of the Gold Eagle. Motioning him forward urgently, Russ gave him no opportunity for delay. "Come on down to the bank, Stevens," he exclaimed. "Right now. Ab Keeler refused to cash Colcord's check, and Crip is down there arguing with him. Maybe we can catch them."

Waving briefly to Sam, Pat started forward. As Cobb had said, they found Keeler and the rancher still warmly arguing the situation. Stevens pushed close coolly. "Howdy, Ab." He nodded to the banker. "What's the trouble here?"

Colcord tried excitedly to tell him, but Pat waved him to silence. He turned expectantly to Keeler. Ab fluttered his pudgy hands. "It's simple, boy. Colcord here has got this check he insists on cashing," the banker said. "I can't get it through his head that I'm unable to recognize it—"

Pat let him talk a few moments longer, following it all closely. "If you're not allowed to honor Colcord's check, it can only be because Stober countermanded payment on it. He can get himself into trouble for that kind of a snide operation. Is that what you're trying to get over without actually saying it, Ab?" he asked finally.

"Not at all." The banker's fleshy jowls grew pink with indignation. "That is, I mean—yes. Stober didn't stop payment on this particular check, you understand. As

I get it he's having a little trouble with his bookkeeper, and asked me to cash no checks till he okayed 'em."

"Today, you mean?" Pat caught him up.

"No, that must've been a week ago at least," was the answer.

Pat's brows rose. "In that case, Stober must have known Colcord would have trouble with this check when he made it out," he stated with care. "Am I right?"

Keeler shrugged. "That I couldn't say, of course. I only know what he said to me," he returned stiffly.

"What kind of trouble was he having with his bookkeeper?" Pat pressed. "Could you make a guess, Ab?"

Keeler hesitated. "I—gathered the man was stealing from him, or juggling the accounts. Some such thing," he allowed finally. "Unauthorized checks, or checks made out in exorbitant amounts, can only amount to that—"

"Not necessarily." Pat shook his head. "If Stober caught the man stealing he could fire him, couldn't he? That wouldn't take a week to straighten out."

"I don't know, Stevens. Stober isn't required to confide in me. He could be trying to recover misappropriated money. I'm not prepared to say," he reminded again.

"Is it the bank's policy to abet this embarrassment of anyone Stober may happen to do business with?" pursued Pat quizzically.

Becoming provoked now, Keeler was not inclined to discuss it further. "No use of your arguin', Stevens! I've got my instructions, and I'm obliged to carry them out until further notice. That's all there is to it." Once more, with finality of manner, he made as if to close the door in their faces.

Pat coolly braced the door back with his foot. "Easy does it, Ab, till we chew this over. Colcord's on the hook and we're trying to ease him out of his jam, remember? He's a depositor of yours too, I understand—in a small way."

Not an essentially unfeeling man, Keeler nodded. "I told Crip to come back at a reasonable hour and I'll consider a loan," he explained patiently.

Pat's headshake was decided. "No, he's got this check

now and there's no reason for him to slap a plaster on Saw Buck." He thought a second. "It happens that I was there when Stober made out the check himself, and I'm satisfied it's good. It better be! Would it make a difference," he inquired, "if I endorsed it for you?"

This time Ab did not even hesitate. "Why not?" he countered shortly. "So long as you know what you're doin', Stevens, you're good for the amount. If you want to spend it that way—"

"Never mind that. I'll undertake to see that Stober honors his own check, no matter what he told you. Get a pen," he directed. "I'll make this check as good as gold —and then you can cash it and keep Colcord happy."

They stepped inside. At the desk Pat endorsed the check, and Keeler accepted it without further demur. It was made out for close to a thousand dollars. Evidently the banker's plea of having locked the vault was an excuse, for he made no difficulty about getting the money at once.

Eyes sparkling, Colcord counted it with care. "Thanks, Stevens! I hope yuh don't have to use a club on Stober —unless yuh already have," he added with perfectly restored humor.

Pat made no direct response. He watched approvingly as Russ Cobb insisted that Colcord stow the money away safely. Then he started out of the place, with a nod for Keeler.

"Say, Stevens!" Colcord followed as hastily as his limp would allow, catching up as they stepped out of the door, rather spitefully slammed and locked behind them by the cashier. Paying no heed, Crip caught Pat by the arm, holding him back. "I aim to do a little business before yuh get away. Could yuh send me over a hundred head of prime Lazy Mare steers right off?"

As it happened it was not particularly convenient for Pat just now. But aware that the events of this day might mean the difference between survival and failure for the old campaigner, he asked exactly what Colcord wanted. They discussed it for a moment, and Pat finally nodded.

"I think I can squeeze that many two-year-olds out for you—"

"Fine. I'll be ready for yuh within the next day or two." The rancher paused. "What are yuh askin', by the way?"

Considering that Pat had been instrumental in seeing that he got redress, he might have left the matter of price to the other's discretion. But the bargaining habit of years was strong. Pat understood. They talked market prices for a minute or two, and it was Pat who took note when young Cobb abruptly started off down the street.

Not long afterward Russ came back with Penny, a smiling and attentive Penny now, who gave the young fellow a flattering attention. Seeing her father she hurried forward.

"Father, were you successful?" she asked with a trace of breathlessness.

Crip nodded, with an expansive smile. "I reckon. This has turned out to be a good stroke of business for us, girl." He swelled with a certain pompous satisfaction, as if privately persuaded that he was still a shrewd dealer.

"That's wonderful," she exclaimed. "I—knew we could depend on Russ."

Pat hid a smile, amused by the readiness of each to assign credit to the person of his own nomination. Old Colcord, he saw, was feeling particularly good. "There wasn't no need of yuh followin' me to town, Daughter," he admonished paternally. "But maybe there's a few things yuh want to pick up while we're here."

"I shouldn't." But she toyed with the temptation, plainly enjoying it. "Perhaps just an item or two? If you'll come with me—"

Colcord allowed himself to be led off. Pat looked after father and daughter with a smile, before turning to Russ. "I hope you'll keep an eye on those kids, and see that they get home okay, Cobb," he suggested dryly.

Russ gave him a dour glance. Concerned as he was about the Colcords, he preferred not to be ribbed about it. Just now he suspected Stevens of a misplaced attempt at humor. "What's the object of that?" he muttered.

Instead of answering Pat nodded significantly upstreet. Cobb turned for a look. To his disgust he saw three or four War Ax punchers loitering in a group before the Gold Eagle. Paying no apparent attention to anyone, and elaborately concerned with their own horseplay, they looked innocent enough. But Russ got it. Chuck Stober normally made such heavy demands on his help that it was by no means usual for a War Ax puncher to appear in town except on an errand. This noticeable departure from custom was therefore probably not without significance.

Russ swallowed hard, nodding soberly. "Makes a difference, don't it?" he murmured darkly. His pause was of the slightest. "I'll keep my eyes open."

Under other circumstances Pat would himself have seen to it that the Colcords came to no harm. This time it suited his design to hand the chore over to the younger man. "Fine. I'll shove along and start gathering that Lazy Mare beef for Crip," he announced.

He left a few minutes later. Cobb lingered on Jeb Winters's store porch, waiting for Colcord and Penny. The girl's item or two must have swelled to a considerable list of needs, for Russ was still impatiently cooling his heels half an hour later when old Crip stepped out of the general store alone.

"Where's Penny?" the puncher asked.

Colcord shrugged, showing a comical disgust. "Yuh know what women are! She picked out a wagon load of fancy grub, and Jeb is deliverin' it to the ranch. She's lookin' at dress goods now!"

"Well, wait a minute," Russ urged when the other started down off the store porch. "You're going to wait for her, aren't you?"

Crip shook his head with a look of stubborn protest. "Another two hours?" he growled half-humorously. "I'd just be in the way, boy. She decided she'd ride out with the rig, now she's satisfied in her mind about me."

Russ found nothing funny in the arrangement. In a

way it suited him to have the girl well out of the way, if
what he half-expected were to come about.

"Are you heading back for the ranch then?" he asked
casually. "I'll go along with you—"

Colcord paused, but the impulse to celebrate was only
fleeting. He nodded. "Might's well," he allowed. "Ain't
nothing more for me here."

Mounting their horses, they started out of town.
Cobb's last backward glance showed him the War Ax
hands still clowning and skylarking before the saloon,
showing no signs of any interest in the activities of others.
The young fellow heaved a mental sigh of relief.

Once on the open trail, Colcord grew garrulous. He
was full of talk now of what he would do with Saw
Buck. True to human nature, he entertained ambitious
plans, most of which would inevitably dissipate with the
morrow. As Russ listened, nevertheless, he found a certain charm in the picture conjured up out of rosy dreams.
He would have given much to follow out Colcord's ambitious designs himself, he thought—with Penny at his
side for encouragement and aid!

The bubble burst sharply twenty minutes later, when
four riders appeared suddenly on the trail a short distance ahead. Cobb hauled up on the reins, peering
keenly. But he already knew. It was the four War Ax
hands whom he had seen in Dutch Springs. As shrewd
suspicion had warned him, they had indeed been on the
watch in town. Seeing Colcord leave, they had promptly taken to horse and circled ahead, making certain of
intercepting the man.

Russ glanced about the circle of the horizon distractedly. Except for themselves and the oncoming punchers it
was empty. War Ax had seen to it that they could look
for no help. Cobb was not foolish enough to attempt
flight. These ruthless warriors would surely overtake them,
with harsher results than if they attempted to brazen
out a meeting.

"Watch yourself, Colcord," he muttered tensely. "This
won't be pleasant. Whatever you do," he added hastily,
"keep your hand away from that gun."

"Huh?" Slower on the uptake, Crip did not immediately grasp the full import of their predicament. "Who are them fellers, boy?"

"Deuce Dimock is one—and the kid puncher, Gyp Carmer, is another," Russ supplied in an undertone as the War Ax hands advanced purposefully. "Look out for that crazy, wild Carmer—he's the most dangerous of the lot."

The approaching quartet spread out as they neared, closing in stony-faced. Cobb reined close to Colcord, facing the roughs with cool defiance. "All right, Dimock. What's this all about?" he rapped.

"Just hand us over the old man," returned Deuce cynically. "We don't want nothin' of you, Cobb—"

"Come on, come on. Pull out of the trail, there!" old Crip broke out fiercely. "Let us by, d' you hear?"

It was Gyp Carmer, the sallow, wicked-eyed kid, who thrust close to grab Colcord's bridle rein. Crip sought angrily to pull away but he was too late.

"Get down, old buck," Carmer invited with thin savagery. "We're havin' a word with yuh—"

"Lay off, Carmer!" Crowding close, Russ unleashed a haymaker that caught the reckless kid wholly unprepared, knocking him out of the saddle to slam to the ground.

For an instant the close-crowding horses reared and jostled, milling together. It was all that saved Cobb. With a shrill imprecation Gyp Carmer sprang up, trying to yank his gun out. He dodged this way and that, firing once wildly—attempting all the while for a clear aim. Letting out a brief roar, Dimock jammed his mount forward, closing in with decision and knocking the kid's gunbarrel down.

"Quit it," Deuce ordered flatly. Sullenly obedient for the moment, the Indian-faced kid crawled aboard his pony, staring with icy venom at Cobb.

"Hang it all! What in tarnation do yuh want?" bawled Colcord, trembling with rage and glaring at the four.

"Just hand over your money, old horse," returned Dimock coolly.

"Ain't got any," Crip spat out.

Deuce laughed rancorously. "That I'll believe—after we get done with yuh," he retorted harshly. "All right, boys. Pull 'em down!" He motioned brusquely to his men.

They closed in with a rush. Cobb suddenly found himself in the center of a swirling melee of fists and elbows. Blows caught him treacherously from behind as he attempted to ward off the attack on Colcord. Fearing only that blazing guns might make their fatal appearance, he swung mightily, jabbing and ducking as he sought to maintain his balance astride the horse.

Bawling at the top of his voice, old Crip suddenly disappeared out of the saddle. Sliding down between the horses, Cobb sought desperately to reach him. He was battered this way and that, iron-shod hoofs flashing close as the broncs tried to break apart. Dimock was yelling angry orders, and Gyp Carmer cursed savagely, crowding forward.

A blinding blow struck Cobb's skull and he wilted, collapsing across Colcord's prone form with the last vestige of defiance beaten out of him.

[12]

No more than half-conscious, Russ felt himself being tumbled roughly aside. Some corner of his brain still attempted to assert itself, but his leaden limbs refused to answer. He heard gruff voices somewhere near at hand. What they said was undistinguishable, until clear words suddenly shocked through him.

"What about Cobb here?" It was the thin, rasping voice of Gyp Carmer. "Better knock him off, eh?"

"Nah. Plenty of time for that," was the unhurried answer. "Stober'll be mad enough now—"

There was more brief muttering. "Nothin' in them saddle pockets?" a voice said sharply. A moment later the dull thud of hoofs came up from the ground under Cobb, a swiftly diminishing sound. After that he was conscious of silence and peace, broken presently by a muffled groan.

It alerted Russ in a twinkling. "That's Colcord," the thought knifed across his foggy brain. Slowly he rolled over, his body heavy and sluggish. It was as much as he could do to force himself to his knees. He blinked through a slowly receding haze.

Old Crip was moving feebly, trying unsuccessfully to raise himself. Forgetting his own dull aches, Russ reached the other man and helped him up. "Are yuh all right, Colcord—?"

Crip managed a nod. Returning rapidly to full possession of his faculties, he darted a fierce glance around. "Why, dang their ornery hides—! What was the idea of tellin' me not to draw a gun on them rowdies, boy?"

Cobb didn't even see the humor of it. "You're alive," he returned tersely. "Neither of us would have been if we tried to shoot it out with those killers. . . . Not that it would make much difference now," he added bitterly.

Colcord paused to look at him. "Why do yuh say that?"

Russ made a passionate gesture. "Look in your pockets, if you haven't found out yet," he retorted doggedly. "All the trouble we went through with that damned check was for nothing!"

Crip started instinctively to feel his pockets, only to halt. A queer look came over his lined cheeks, melting into a crooked grin. "Is that what's botherin' yuh?" he declared. "Shucks, boy. Them crooks never got that money!"

"They didn't?" A ton weight suddenly seemed to roll off Cobb's back. "They must have, Colcord! Are you dead sure—?"

Crip began to laugh. "Cripes, yes. I—" Again he broke off, only to chuckle more richly. "Yuh mean yuh thought I was carryin' that money all the time? Why,

Penny wanted to do some more shoppin' there in town
—so I handed her my wad. Told her to see it got home
safe. Them tough roosters was never anywhere near that
money, son!"

Now that it was all over, the puncher's blood ran
cold at the thought of their narrow escape. At the same
time deep anger stirred in him. He glanced hastily about.
Their horses were waiting patiently a short distance
away, reins dragging on the ground. There was no sign
whatever of the War Ax hands. Yet this did not relieve
his deep apprehension in the slightest.

"We're in luck," he got out slowly. "And I don't believe in crowdin' it. Shall we shove on to Saw Buck while
we can still make it?"

The adventure over, Colcord regained his cocky
aplomb almost at once. "I'm on my way home," he
assented. "But there ain't no infernal rush. Let me get this
kink out of my bad leg—"

He hobbled about unhurriedly, expressing himself freely concerning the would-be robbers. "Somethin'll have
to be done about them riffraff punchers Stober and some
of the other big ranchers are pickin' up," he complained
dourly. "It's gettin' so it ain't safe for anybody no more!"

Cobb listened inattentively, impatient to be gone. He
still could not understand how it happened that Colcord's life had been spared. It was not impossible that
the chagrined renegades might yet return to complete
their work.

"Come on, will you?" he rasped irritably. "We'll both
be a lot safer if we get out of here."

"What's your hurry?" Shrugging, the rancher complied with a show of tolerance. "Shove along by yourself,
boy, if yuh can't wait. I ain't so young as I was once," he
growled his humorous protest.

Ignoring this, Russ waited till the other man pulled himself laboriously astride his horse. They set off. Glancing
back over the empty trail, Cobb wanted nothing better
than to seek Penny out and remain with her jealously. But
he knew his duty was to make sure that her father got
safely home.

Despite his uneasiness, nothing else of note occurred during the ride to Saw Buck. Colcord voiced a long rambling monologue on the way, explaining in detail what he would do with renegade punchers in general if he had his way. Russ knew it for one of those heated diatribes which never came to anything. Reaching the ranch, old Crip dismounted to move about gingerly, still stiff from his battering. Cobb occupied himself with off-saddling for the rancher and turning the bronc into a corral. That done, he gave no sign of an intention to depart.

"Thought yuh was in a sweat," Colcord barked at him.

"I am." Refusing to explain, Russ moved away to a point from which he could watch the Dutch Springs trail. It seemed a long time before he observed a rig advancing across the range at what seemed an unconscionably leisurely pace. Shortly afterward he discerned Taze Cromwell, Winters's toothless deliveryman, seated on the wagon with Penny Colcord by his side. The two were conversing amicably, and all seemed well.

As they rode into the ranch yard the girl stared at Russ's face. His jaw showed a long bruise, and he had obviously been in a mix-up. "What's this?" she asked, turning to examine her father. "I hope you two haven't been fighting—"

Colcord grinned with unaccustomed spirit, but Cobb thrust the matter aside. "Did you bring that money home safe, Penny?" he demanded sharply.

She looked at him in surprise. "Of course. Why shouldn't I?" As she spoke she made sure of her pocketbook and waited for the reply. But Cobb had learned all he wanted to know.

"All right. Put it in a good place, because you'll be needing it shortly." He turned to his horse with a decisive movement.

"But Russ—" She was even more mystified than before. "Must you go so soon?"

He jerked a nod. "I'll be back. Right now I got business."

Even Colcord was a shade doubtful of his meaning, frowning as he watched the young fellow ride away. Russ knew it would be a good ten minutes before the girl got the story of their experience from her father, if at all. Would she guess his object?

"It can't make any difference," he told himself soberly. "I can't even be sure Colcord got the connection with War Ax! All the same, Stober better have a good story ready!"

Leaving Saw Buck behind, he headed straight for War Ax and rode into the big main ranch boldly. Men were about the bunkhouses and corrals as usual. He found it a good sign that neither Deuce Dimock nor young Carmer appeared to be here.

"Stober around?" Russ asked a ranch hand carelessly, tethering his bronc.

The man thumbed toward the house, not bothering to stop. Cobb turned that way, seeking out the owner's tiny adobe office, and knocking at the screen door.

"Being awful polite, ain't you?" a heavy voice grated from within as Cobb pulled the screen open and stepped through. "Well. You, eh? You show up on payday anyway, don't you?"

Ignoring this curt reference to his recent absence from the ranch, Russ spoke up determinedly. "Mr. Stober, we've got to have a talk."

Stober promptly shook his head, cocking a satirical eyebrow. "No raises, Cobb. We might as well understand each other."

Russ found it heavy going in his effort to strike straight to the point. He took the bit in his teeth and plunged on. "I know you gave Crip Colcord a check for his cattle," he stated flatly. "As it happens, I saw the old fellow cash it. I was with him when Dimock and Carmer made their play to get the money back!"

Chuck regarded him with a frown, leaning back in his creaking swivel chair. "How's that again?" He spoke almost casually. Then his tone sharpened. "What in the world *are* you talkin' about—?"

Cobb shook his head. "Since you pretend not to have

heard yet—and that is barely possible—I'll tell you." He gave a straight account of the encounter on the trail with the War Ax hands led by Deuce Dimock.

"What!" Stober showed incredulous astonishment before he had heard even half of the story. "You mean that old fool promptly lost the whole amount less than a day after I saw to it that he was paid?"

"No, I don't mean anything of the kind." Listening acutely, Russ was weighing the rancher's every word for the first false note. "I mean that Dimock tried to relieve him of it!"

"But they didn't get it, eh?" Stober's show of relief was masterly. "Good! I expect some of the credit is yours for saving his hide—"

Russ denied the accomplishment. "No, I got the same treatment myself—as you can see," he confessed flatly. "I'm not crazy enough yet to pull a gun on four fools. The only thing that saved *him* was that he wasn't carrying the money at the time."

Except for the alertness with which he listened, Stober's reaction to the news was unreadable. "You don't mean you was carryin' it for him—?"

"I mean neither of us had it."

Stober scratched an ear thoughtfully. "I still don't get my connection with this—disgraceful affair," he rumbled, watching Cobb steadily. "Why are you tellin' me about it?"

"Blast it all!" burst out Russ, uncertainty in his manner despite his firmness. "When you hand over a fat check under protest, and then your own hands make a rough play to get the money back—!"

Chuck interrupted with a grating laugh. "I see." There was a derisive glint in his eye. "I suppose it *could* be looked at that way." His face turned cold then. "You didn't lose much time throwing this at me, did you?"

Cobb grew increasingly exasperated at the smoothness with which this man parried his every accusing implication. "Now tell me you didn't know a thing about it!" he exclaimed tightly.

"Why bother? You don't want to believe me anyway.

I'm only the man who pays your salary," Stober jibed thinly. "As a matter of fact, though—how could my boys know I'd paid Colcord a handsome sum? I don't exactly advertise such things—"

"Unless with a definite purpose in mind. Is that it?" The biting retort flashed through Russ's mind, but he held it back, instinct warning him that Stober was far shrewder than he had ever supposed.

"Another thing," Chuck pursued hardily. "*You* may think I'm fool enough to send my own hands on such an errand—supposing I had any such idea in mind!" he said contemptuously. "Would we be simple enough to pick a time when another of my employees was on hand to act as a witness?"

Swallowing hard, Cobb felt obliged to acknowledge the force of the argument. He had to admit that Stober was using hard sense. "Then what in blazes were they thinkin' of?" he demanded desperately.

Stober shrugged. "Who knows? Maybe a poker game —or a big drunk! I don't pretend to name every scheme that floats through the heads of my men." Surely he found the logical answer for every attack. "Most likely they had a drink or two under their belts and were out for a good time. . . . I'll call Dimock to account, of course," he continued carelessly. "I won't stand for rowdy work. But so long as my work gets done I can't ask too much of these men. It's all I've got the right to ask from you," he hinted pointedly. "Or you'd be busy explaining where you've been lately!"

There was more talk; but as he stepped out of the office a short time later, Cobb knew the taste of defeat.

"I don't believe a bit of it," he thought angrily, returning to his horse and starting about the work Stober had brusquely outlined for him. "The man's guilty, and brazen about it! I didn't think quick enough to throw that stampede in his teeth. Blast him, he tried a trick on Colcord and got caught in the act. Why couldn't it have happened the same way a second time?"

Russ was not so dull that he didn't realize his own precarious position. "If I make an enemy of Stober it'll be Dad he'll strike at next, instead of either Colcord or me!" Strongly inclined as he was to quit his job, the thought made him go slow, though it could not sway his anxious thinking.

An hour after dark, when his work was done, Russ rode into Antler. Finding old Ben in the midst of supper, he joined him without comment. Not till they were done eating did either speak.

"So what did yuh hear today?" the elder asked gruffly.

"Hear? What about?"

"Has Stober made Colcord an offer for Saw Buck yet?" Ben asked cynically.

Russ grunted. "Why, no. Crip wouldn't consider it if he did!"

Cobb took this with a grain of salt. "He'll have t' do somethin' mighty quick—losin' all that stock. No point in waitin' till the ax falls. . . . Ha! That's a good one," he chuckled over his own pun. "Till the ax falls—War Ax, that is!"

Russ frowned his annoyance. "Little danger of that," he said coolly. Without thinking he plunged into an account of how Sheriff Lawlor's intervention had resulted in a check made out to Colcord covering his full loss.

Old Cobb listened with growing anger. Suddenly his open mouth snapped shut. "Are yuh tellin' me that old devil is no worse off than ever?" he ripped out furiously.

Half-ashamed of his father's narrow prejudices, Russ sought a means to jolt him. "He's probably better off, if anything," he retorted shortly.

Jumping up from the table, Ben raved and ranted intemperately while he sought agitatedly for pipe and tobacco. "Hang it, boy! To hear you talk, a feller'd believe you're on *his* side, not mine," he fumed. "Is it tha girl again? Because, by gravy, I'll do somethin' about it!'

Not till he had his pipe going, his grizzled head wreathed in an angry cloud of smoke, did he start to simmer down. Entertaining radically different ideas, bu without an ounce of proof to back them up, Russ prudently preserved an austere silence. Old Ben couldn' leave it alone, nagging at him irritably for an hour before stamping off to bed.

In the morning Russ got away to his work without seeing his parent. But, his concern awakened, he saw to it that he was back at Antler several times during the next two days, keeping an eye on Ben and making sure everything was all right.

It was thus not entirely by accident that on the afternoon of the second day he came across old Cobb, sourly watching a cloud of dust rolling into the sky from across the line on Colcord's Saw Buck. Ben noted his son's arrival absently.

"What in creation is that?" He waved a gnarled hand toward the brown, billowing scroll, though he must have guessed.

Russ glanced that way briefly. "Must be the herd Crip ordered from Pat Stevens to restock with," he said briefly.

Cobb's response was not entirely unexpected. He snorted and swore, venting his envious exasperation without restraint. Russ listened until he was tired of it, then turned to ride away. He did not go far, however, pausing in convenient cover to watch what his father did.

For a brief time Russ was puzzled. After making sure he was alone, as he thought, old Ben dismounted. He was in an isolated spot, close to his own range line. Kneeling, he fussed about the edge of the dry brush, poking here and there. Russ watched this briefly, then his breath sucked in. Wheeling his bronc, he tore back at top speed.

He was barely in time to leap to the ground and, thrusting the older man roughly aside, to stamp out the small blaze his parent had set alight in several places. Only when all danger of its spreading was past did he turn on Cobb savagely.

"Dad, have you gone clean out of your head? Only a maniac would deliberately set fire to the open range," he whipped out condemningly. "You're damned lucky it was me and not somebody else who saw this!"

Fully aware that argument would be of no avail, Ben acted much like a sullen boy caught in a particularly flagrant caper. Russ had no patience whatever with him. "Get yourself on home," he yelled bitterly. "If you can't act like a man, I'll have to. Go on—git!"

Humbly, without a word, his father crawled astride his pony and headed for the ranch. Not till he was certain of this did Russ turn the other way and strike out purposefully for Colcord's Saw Buck.

[13]

Driving the carefully selected Lazy Mare herd onto Saw Buck, Pat Stevens found it expedient as a part of his delivery to see that they were turned out on good grass.

"Better hold the stuff pretty well bunched," he called over to Ezra and Sam, who had come along with the drive. "Colcord will want to rebrand before they get mixed with his own beef. I'll shove along and tell him we're here."

"Hurry it up, will yuh, Stevens?" Wiping his sweaty face with upraised arm, Sloan grinned at his younger friend disarmingly. "This ain't no picnic."

"No—and you're no young girl in pigtails, either," retorted Pat unfeelingly.

Turning his horse, he trotted briskly out of the dusty melee. Before he had covered a thousand yards in the direction of Colcord's ranch, however, he learned that their arrival had been observed. Kip McKinley, the elderly Saw Buck puncher, came forward on his pony to meet him.

"By cracky, Stevens! That's a fine sight," the old fellow quavered, gazing toward the Lazy Mare stock. "Must be partin' with your finest strain there. If old Crip don't kiss yuh for this, I will!"

Pat laughed. There could be no doubting the gnarled rawhide's gratification over his employer's good fortune. "Be careful what you say, Kip," he retorted jestingly.

"I may just turn around and drive the stuff home after a threat like that."

Turning in side by side, they pushed on to the ranch. Penny Colcord stepped out of the door as they neared, awaiting their advance. "You're here, Pat!" she exclaimed warmly. "Dad will be glad—"

He nodded. "Where is he?"

"Right here I be!" Before the girl could answer, Crip emerged from the house, hopping awkwardly as he pulled on his second boot. He straightened up, flushed and expectant. "Brought that bunch of steers with yuh, Stevens, I hope?"

"Well, now, he sure did! Wait till yuh toss your eye over them beeves, boss," interposed Kip enthusiastically.

"Uh-huh." Nodding, Colcord accepted it as proved, and was about to move hastily toward the corral for a mount when Stevens halted him.

"Sorry, Colcord," he said practically. "But under the circumstances I'll have to ask for my money now. Might as well settle it while we're here at the house, eh?"

"Sure," Crip agreed readily. Distractedly slapping his pockets as if expecting to find the sum on him, he paused. "What was that amount again—?"

Pat named the figure they had agreed on. It was sufficiently modest that, after paying it, Colcord would still have some working capital left.

Crip nodded absently, collecting his wits. "Let's see." He glanced at Penny. "Yuh gave that money to me and I put it away, didn't I?" Suddenly he grinned. "Don't mind me, Stevens. I ain't always as excited as this. It's in the house. I'll get it."

Hobbling to the door, he stepped in. Penny shook her head faintly at Pat, with an indulgent smile. "You've managed to please him, you see," she said.

Pat looked at her, frowning. "I hope you don't think I'm grasping, Penny." He scarcely knew how to explain that he sought to remove temptation from men to whom the smell of loose money was as sugar to wild bees.

"Not at all." She looked surprised. "Dad thoroughly expects to pay for whatever cattle he purchases—"

The sound of a heavy thud from the house, like a chair falling, broke in on their talk. They heard a strangled cry, and the dull thump of old Crip's boots as he stumbled toward the door. A moment later he barged out with the most tortured and outraged expression on his face Pat had ever seen.

"It's gone—the money's gone!" he bawled furiously. "It was here! Somebody took it!"

"Oh—Dad!" Running to him, the girl threw her arms about him imploringly. "That can't be true. It's—impossible! Surely you must have forgotten where you tucked it—?"

There was an agony of apprehension in her voice. Even Colcord paused, struck with the vague possibility, and struggling at the same time with cruel doubt. But Pat was not deceived. His usually unmoved countenance grew grave.

"There can't be any question about this, Colcord?" he queried.

Shaking, suddenly an old man once more, Crip made an eloquent gesture. "I know where *I* put it," he brought out desperately. "It ain't there now." Suddenly he whirled on the girl, who had released him to walk back and forth distractedly. "You, Penny!" There was thunder in his voice, and suspicion as well. "Who's been around here in the last two days, besides you and Kip and me?"

His forceful air demanded an answer. Penny looked from him to Pat beseechingly, trying to think. Suddenly she blanched. "Why—nobody. . . . That is, nobody but Russ Cobb. He—stopped for a visit yesterday. But he wouldn't—" She broke off sharply, watching Colcord's face with growing alarm. *"Father!* You surely don't think—"

"Cobb, eh? Why, the young whelp!" Crip bellowed furiously.

It so chanced that Russ himself rode round the corner of the house at that moment. He was in time to hear a part of the girl's words and Colcord's impassioned response. One keen glance at these faces warned him of just how serious the situation was.

"All right. Here I am." He spoke with quiet firmness. "What have I been up to now?"

"Nothing, Russ," Penny replied hurriedly in the heavy silence. "The money Dad received from Mr. Stober seems to have been mislaid and—" She could carry her calm pretense no further, her breath catching.

"So I took it, eh?" Russ got his tight opening words out, his jaws corded. "Go ahead—say it!" Suddenly he was yelling, glaring angrily at Colcord. "You had it on the tip of your tongue just as I got here—!"

"Well, now—" began Crip confusedly, already a bit ashamed of his haste.

But Russ was not to be appeased. "Never mind then! We both know what you're thinking," he cried hotly. "It was a sorry day for me when I first laid eyes on either of you! I tried to save your money—so this is my pay!"

"Russ," exclaimed Penny urgently as he yanked his pony around and started impetuously away. Cobb either did not hear her or refused to heed, not turning his head. Colcord cursed to relieve his taut feelings.

"Kind of hot, ain't he?" he complained peevishly.

Pat had found nothing to say, being slow to meddle with a situation not his own before making up his mind. He spoke up now. "It was bad luck having Cobb ride up just when he did," he allowed quietly. "From his actions, Colcord, you can't persuade me he had anything to do with it. I'll let him cool off a minute or two but—" He picked up his reins. "Maybe it wouldn't be a bad idea, before this goes too far, if I reminded him he was the one who accused himself."

"If you only would." Penny's small voice said that she could not wholly acquit herself in the matter. "Why did I ever bother to mention his being here—?"

"Take it easy." Pat's level smile held more assurance than he could have found ready words to support. "I'll have a try at the boy, anyway." He started away.

Cobb's anger had carried him beyond sight of Saw Buck at a brisk clip, but the bitter perplexity of his thoughts soon slowed him down. "How could Penny believe such a thing?" he groaned, forgetting in his dismay that he was entirely lacking proof that she condemned him.

"Well, Cobb. You sure flew off the handle and no mistake!" a calm voice broke through his gloomy absorption. Russ whirled to find Pat Stevens near at hand, regarding him quizzically.

"Go ahead—rub it in!" he snapped.

Pat shook his head. "No, I won't. You may have that money in your pocket now, of course," he continued easily. "I'll never believe it till you tell me yourself. But maybe you remember something."

"Oh? What would I be likely to remember?"

"What you didn't get there in time to hear," proceeded Pat placidly, "was Colcord asking Penny who had been at the ranch during the past two days."

"And she named me!"

Pat smiled thinly. "There, weren't you?" Cobb reluctantly nodded. "So what I'm asking you now is who else you might have seen around," Pat caught him up.

Russ frowned. "There wasn't anybody but—" he began, then halted. "That's foolish, of course. . . . But Stevens, I *did* nearly run into Gyp Carmer over here on the edge of Saw Buck!" He spoke crisply now, eyes glinting. "You don't suppose by any remote chance—"

"What was he doing?"

Cobb shrugged. "Carmer's a shifty hombre. Whether he spotted me or not I couldn't figure out. He disappeared awful quick! I lost him after that—"

Pat weighed this. He was acquainted with Gyp Carmer by repute and casual observation. The sullen-faced kid puncher had made no favorable impression. "Would you say he was capable of sneaking into Colcord's place?" he asked keenly.

Russ scoffed. "Think of somethin' hard, Stevens!"

"Would he be likely to have a chance—from what you've seen over there?"

Cobb's nod came more slowly. "He'd have had his chance the day I was over there," he admitted. "Penny and I left the house empty for half an hour. Colcord and old Kip were gone."

"Nobody else you can recall seeing anywhere around?" inquired Pat carefully.

Russ thought this over, then shook his head. "I won't even swear Carmer was close enough to really count," he said.

Pat sifted the available evidence and reached his decision with characteristic promptness. "Where would we be likely to find Carmer right now?"

Russ had the answer to that one ready. "If I was him, and I suddenly turned up with a wad of money in my pocket—you'd find me in some saloon," he said positively.

"Good answer." Pat grinned. "We'll say for the argument, then, that *if* Gyp Carmer latched onto Colcord's cash, he's probably in town right now. Shall we head for there?"

Cobb hesitated. "Ganado or Dutch Springs?"

"Ganado's closest. We can try there first, and if we don't find him we'll shove on."

This was more than satisfactory to Russ. "You understand that we may find nothing at all," he reminded Pat soberly as they turned their faces toward town. "We're both guessing, Stevens. But I'll go to any lengths if there's a bare chance of clearing this up."

Pat did not need to be reminded of how he felt. "Me too. We're in this together, Cobb," he replied simply. "Unless we find it, I stand a good chance of not getting my money."

Russ shook his head. "That's a heap different," he argued stubbornly. "You don't know what it is to be called a thief. Not till it happens to you—"

Stevens only smiled. In his day he had been branded a killer and worse, and had lived to tell the tale. Yet he knew how real this predicament was to Cobb.

It was close to midday by the time they reached Ganado. While no larger than Dutch Springs, this mining supply town had the appearance of being far busier and more prosperous. Men crowded the streets and freight rigs and teams were moving about. Although they were forced to maintain a sharper watch, this activity enabled them to ride in and rack their broncs without any particular attention being paid them.

"Gyp'll be holdin' forth in some bar if he's here at all," Cobb declared, glancing along the street as they stretched their legs.

There were no less than six or seven saloons in Ganado, not counting the lower class dives, all vying for the trade of celebrating miners and teamsters. Pat only nodded. "Take one side of the street, and I'll take the other," he proposed. "If you spot Carmer give a yell before you move in."

Cobb's assent was tight. "You do the same. It's all I ask, Stevens."

Separating, they took different sides of the main drag and systematically combed the bars. Russ visited two places without result and his blood pressure was down to zero. Suddenly it seemed to him insane that they might hope to locate Gyp Carmer so casually, even were he to prove the thief. He tramped out of the Miners Rest with his hopes plummeting, and headed doggedly for the Palace Saloon, the last place of any consequence on this side of the street.

The Palace was an elaborate establishment, built practically on stilts in front, with long flights of wooden steps running up to the porch. Behind its ornate facade the notorious dive clung like a bird's-nest to the rocky ribs of the canyonside. Russ ran up the steps quickly to the plank porch. The front windows of the place were long and narrow, reaching nearly to the floor and affording an unusually good view of the interior. Heading for the batwings, Cobb glanced perfunctorily through the nearest window, and suddenly dodged aside. Nerves tight as a bowstring, he paused to gather his wits.

Against all expectation, Carmer was inside, clearly enjoying himself to the hilt and already so tipsy that it seemed unlikely he was bothering to note anything or anyone about him. Fierce anger surged through Russ. He fought down the impulse to rush in and collar the vicious puncher on the spot.

Reaching the porch rail beyond view of the bar windows, he feverishly scanned the busy street below. Stevens was nowhere in sight. Muffling an exclamation, Russ sprang to the nearest steps and ran down. As luck had it, he had not gone twenty feet in the street before Pat appeared.

"What luck, Cobb?" he said swiftly.

Russ pointed upward. "He's there," he got out tersely, curbing his rising excitement. Hitching his cartridge belt around, Pat glanced upward briefly at the Palace and started that way with Cobb at his side.

Climbing the steps steadily, they reached the top and headed for the door. Pat pushed through first. Forced behind him momentarily, Russ followed at once and halted two steps inside. His eyes widened. While five minutes ago the place had presented a scene of easy revelry, with Gyp Carmer a prominent figure, it was now as somnolent and dull as the day before payday. Carmer himself was nowhere to be seen.

A man knocked the roulette ball about idly in its track, and another dozed at one of the card tables. Two men murmured with their heads together at the end of the bar, while the sleek-headed bartender absently polished a glass. Looking the setup over, Stevens started coolly for the rear of the place.

"Where yuh goin'?"

It was the barkeep. Halting, Pat turned to survey him deliberately. He did not reply, going on toward the back. Less assured than the tall, wide-shouldered man in the lead, Cobb followed alertly, a hand on his gun butt. The bartender measured this situation with heavy eyes and decided he wanted no part of it. He said no more.

A hall opened in back of the bar, running toward an ell. Pat moved into it. Small rooms, probably for cards, opened off on either side. All the doors were open at this hour except one, and it was toward this that Stevens made his way with Russ close at his shoulder.

The door was locked. A single kick made it spring open, shuddering. Pat saw Gyp Carmer staggering forward, a half-filled bottle upraised as if to strike. Russ sprang through to bat it nimbly aside. With a bellow

Carmer lunged at him. But he was more than half-drunk, and his faculties were dulled. Cobb unleashed a single powerful jab that sent Gyp reeling wildly and crashing down with a whining groan. He started to struggle up, heaving desperately. Russ gave him a brutal thrust that tumbled him over flat on his stomach. Kneeling, Cobb planted a sturdy knee in the small of his back, holding him pinned.

"Okay, Stevens. I've drawn his fangs," he snapped. "Go through his pockets, will you? If we have to we'll take him apart and see what he's made of!"

Complying methodically, Pat pulled pocket after pocket inside out without finding a thing. Cobb watched this with hunted eyes, his desperate hope waning by the moment. Stevens was grunting over the last empty pocket when Russ abruptly rose and lunged toward Carmer's hat, which had tumbled half-a-dozen feet away when he first fell. Cobb got it. Straightening up, his eyes ablaze, he held out the battered Stetson.

"Look at this!"

Inside the crown, stuffed behind the stained sweat-band, could be seen thin, crumpled wads of currency. Carmer's ingenious cache for his loot had been found.

[14]

"By golly, Stevens! You were right," Russ exclaimed, tearing the loose bills out of Carmer's hat. "That is, if we can be sure this is Colcord's money—"

Pat grunted. "Where else would he get it? Count what you've got there, Cobb. We can soon tell."

Russ ran through the bills and named an amount it was highly unlikely any cowpuncher would come by honestly. Pat nodded. "It's within a hundred of what Crip had," he declared. "We know Penny spent some—

and Carmer must have dropped a few dollars getting that load on."

Handing the money over, Russ wiped his hands on his pant-legs as if ridding himself of something unclean. His glance at Gyp Carmer was disdainful. "Shall we get out of here?"

Leaving the card room, they moved back through the Palace the way they had come. Glowering looks met them in the bar, but there was no attempt to halt them. Pausing in the outside door to glance behind him, Pat looked his unspoken warning and stepped out. He and Cobb clattered down the high steps to the street.

Neither spoke till they reached their horses. Pat paused there, looking across at the young fellow. "It'll be a pleasure for you to return this money to Colcord and tell him about it, Russ." He started to return it.

To his faint surprise Russ held up his hand. "Not me," he ruled decidedly. "I've had enough. It was you that tracked it down anyway, Stevens," he pursued strictly. "I'll shove along home."

"Whatever you say." Pat swung into the saddle, yet still he delayed, his brows puckered. "You owe it to Penny to give her a chance to explain that she was defending you, really," he observed mildly.

"Old Crip wasn't," retorted Cobb tartly. "He'll know when you tell him. But I want this to sink in awhile. Then maybe next time he won't be so quick on the trigger."

Pat had never pretended to give advice in such affairs. "You're the doctor," he returned with a smile. "But I still think Penny's an awful nice girl, Russ—"

"You don't have to tell me," flashed Cobb. Giving the other a dark look, he hauled his bronc around and trotted off the street. Pat let him go, following more leisurely. At the first restaurant he sensibly pulled up to go in for his dinner, and as a consequence did not see Cobb strike the open range at the mouth of the canyon and head straight across the swells for Antler.

The truth was, the puncher was both bewildered and dismayed by his own mixed luck. "Penny's always glad to see me over there," he mused bleakly. Yet had he not visited the girl at Saw Buck he would never have been involved in this latest tangle.

Over and above that, however, was his growing suspicion of Chuck Stober's part in recent events. "Gyp Carmer couldn't have known about Colcord's money unless he was told—and who else would have told him?" he asked himself. "It's the second time War Ax hands made a play for that money. How much of an accident could that be?"

Nearing home, he jerked to attention at the distant crack of a gun. In town no one paid much attention to an occasional shot; but on the range gunfire had a meaning. Hauling up, Russ listened carefully. Two minutes later it came again—a double explosion, followed by a third, sounding more distant.

As near as Cobb could determine the shots came from the direction of the Antler ranch house. He tightened up in a twinkling. So far as he knew, only his father could be there. What did it mean? Clapping spurs to the bronc he set off at a sharp canter, with growing alarm.

His first glimpse of the ranch house across the brushy swells told him nothing. Still a quarter-mile away, the fresh clap of guns only served to increase his speed. Setting a course straight for the house, he was covering ground fast when an angry bee buzzed past close to his face.

When it was followed by a second, whining even closer, Cobb swerved sharply aside into a depression. He knew now what he was up against. Whoever was out there hiding in the brushy cover was besieging the Antler house and, having spotted his approach, was determined to drive him off before he could get into the fight.

Cursing himself for having ridden out the last few days without a rifle in his saddle boot, Russ drew his Colt and examined it briefly. If he wondered whether the attackers would allow him to pull away unmolested, he had his answer a moment later.

"Over this way! He ain't gone far!" a harsh cry floated to him across the brush.

A carbine cracked more loudly, and a slug clipped fragments from the brush off at one side. The would-be assassin had his position figured pretty close. Dismounting, Russ looked about hastily. Toward the west this depression led toward a draw. Leading his pony, he hurried that way, not remounting till he was well below the level of the surrounding range.

Swinging up then, and bending forward over the horn, he urged his mount down the meandering draw. He had not covered a hundred yards before a gun crashed from somewhere behind. He had been sighted, and his attacker was pumping shot after shot. A shot or two went wild before Cobb felt something tug at his foot. A slug had torn half of his stirrup-guard away. A second twitched his shirtsleeve, and he felt a brief burn on his upper arm. Another snarled close overhead.

"Jumping Jerusalem! Let's get out of here!"

At the first shot Russ had hurled his mount to the left toward the side of the winding draw. The long minute before he reached effective cover seemed endless. Sweeping a look around, he saw that he was safe for the moment. He heard cries from behind him, but he could make out no words.

He dashed madly for the next elbow turn in the draw, and made it. Recklessly hurling the bronc sidewise into an intersecting draw, he plunged forward with undiminished speed. Gradually the wash climbed upward, forcing him toward open range. Yet he must chance it. He clambered out of the dwindling wash, the loose dirt flying behind him, and flashed a look about. No one at all was in sight at the moment. Russ spotted another wash and dived into it, driving the bronc without mercy as the deepening depression straggled off in a fresh direction.

Riding as fast as he could for more than ten minutes, keeping to cover and confusing his trail as thoroughly as possible, Cobb finally felt that he had thrown off pursuit, at least for a time. He did not slack off, working steadily in a wide circle toward the rising foothills. Not again did he find danger close on his heels. But from time to time he heard the continuing pound of spiteful gunfire. Someone back there was either trying to drive Ben Cobb from his home, or to kill him.

It only increased Russ's savage determination to take a hand in this fight. Reaching the hills, he faded into their folds with the ease of long familiarity. Ten minutes later he was working down toward the flat on which Antler lay. He could hear the persistent crack of guns plainly now, and even made out the occasional slap of a slug against the cabin.

Leaving his pony concealed in dense brush thirty yards from the house, he crawled on till he reached the rear of the barn. At its rear corner he halted, fearing his father might take him for an enemy. Ben would be so keyed up that he was likely to shoot first and look afterward.

"Hey, Pop!" he called as loudly as he dared.

There was no response. An occasional detonation from the front of the house told him that Ben was grimly intent on fighting off his assailants. Picking up a half-pound rock, Russ heaved it at the back door. It bounced off with a hollow crash.

It must have been heard. After a delay a wooden shutter rattled and a cautious hail came. "Who is that—?" It wasn't his father's voice. Even in the tension of the moment Russ realized that much. Yet he took a chance.

"It's Russ—Russ Cobb," he called, making sure not to show himself as he cupped his hands to his mouth. "Open the back door and I'll make a run for it!"

Following a still longer wait, the door jarred and began to swing back. A man showed himself briefly in the aperture. With a grunt of relief Russ recognized Ezra.

"Look out, Ez! Here I come!"

Leaping into the open, Cobb sprinted across the yard toward the house. Even now Ezra was taking no chances. He peered keenly with his one eye, Colt in hand, holding the door ajar till he made out who it was. Then the door swung back. Running full-tilt, Russ burst in and turned to slam the door shut behind him.

"Hey! Somebody took a pot at yuh." Ezra stared at him sharply. "You're all bloody, boy—'

Russ was surprised now to note the blood that had soaked his hanging sleeve. He felt nothing, and the shallow flesh wound he had sustained certainly did not impair his efficiency. "That was a while back, Ez," he supplied carelessly. "Those hombres tried to stop me out on the range. What's going on here, anyway?"

Ez hesitated. "Hanged if I know, for sure! Me and Sam was on our way home from Saw Buck when some blackleg blasted away at us—"

Russ looked at him in amazement. "So you're the ones that led those killers here?" he exclaimed deeply.

"Hold your horses, will yuh!" roared Ez. "Whoever it is out there, they was smokin' Antler when we come along. They tried to drive us off. Good thing we wouldn't let 'em. Your dad's already been hit!"

On hearing this, Russ promptly turned away, making for the front room of the cabin. It was dusky inside, with everything closed up and the wooden storm shutters pulled to for added protection. But Russ made out Sam Sloan, crouching before a window, rifle in hand, while his father moved restlessly to and fro.

"Dad! What started this racket?" burst out Russ tensely. "Who's out there, do you know?"

Cobb whirled toward him brusquely. "Got here finally, did yuh?" he rasped. "Must've come in through a gopher hole if yuh don't even know what's goin' on. It's Crip Colcord throwin' lead at us, o' course! Who would it be?"

"Dad! Are you dead sure of this—?"

Ben did not answer. His rifle at the ready, the old wildcat prowled from one shuttered window to another as he spat muttered curses to himself. His shirt had been pulled off, and Russ saw that one shoulder was bandaged, high up. It could not hinder his restless energy. Sure that he understood this unprovoked and violent attack thoroughly, Cobb was boiling with rage.

"Aw, now—" Ezra sought to appease him gruffly. "Me and Sam was out there before we made it in, and *we* never saw Colcord at all!"

Cobb waved a disposing hand. "Course yuh didn't!" he flared. "Be a fool to show himself, wouldn't he?"

Sam turned where he knelt at the window to glance at Russ, shaking his head pityingly. It was a tacit confession that the partners fully understood Cobb's fixation about his neighbor, without being able to argue Ben out of it.

A buzzing slug crashed through the slab door, causing Ezra to duck aside. Russ impatiently pulled his parent back away from the danger area. "All right! Watch what you're doing before you lose a leg," he barked.

Ben shook him off, glowering. There was a muffled rattle of gunfire outside, and lead peppered the sturdy log front of the house. It prompted them all to make for a window or some other aperture, ready to fight off a determined assault at need. A lively exchange ensued, but the attack did not materialize.

"Whole trouble is, I ain't rightly seen one of them louses yet," sang out Sam, in exasperation. "So far, I been pluggin' away at puffs of gunsmoke there in the brush!" He triggered a shot and withdrew the rifle, grumbling.

"We can fight 'em off all afternoon and not get anywhere," Russ seconded uneasily. "I ran into a couple of them. Alone, I couldn't do anything but run for it—"

"Four of us here now," grunted Ez. "They're awful tough if they try rushin' the place!"

"We're fools to be stayin' here and takin' it," interjected Sam. "Why can't we steal out there somehow and stir up a real ruckus?"

Old Cobb promptly vetoed the proposal. "Ain't possible to get away from here on horseback without bein' spotted," he growled. "Show ourselves, and we'll be picked off like sittin' brush hens!"

A silence fell to the accompaniment of intermittent firing. All were busily weighing the situation.

"Maybe that's the angle for us to work on," brought out Russ soberly. "Nobody would figure us crazy enough to barge into a range fight on foot. We could stick close together, and be on top of them before they suspected a thing!"

"Hey! Now you're talkin'." Stout as he was, Sloan had never been short on energy. "Yuh must know every wrinkle of this range around here, boy. We can crawl out there and blow 'em off the face of the earth!"

"Pure foolishness," snorted Ben vigorously. After a moment he added: "But if it'll help lay Colcord by the heels, it's worth a try. Let's get goin'—"

"Nope." Ezra had been thinking shrewdly. "Not you, Cobb. It'll take us twenty minutes to sneak out there where we can operate. Somebody's got to stay here and keep 'em busy. With that sore shoulder, you're elected."

Ben read what it meant. If the renegades stormed the house while he was here alone, he would not last long. But with all his failings, he had never been accused of lack of nerve. His nod was curt. "Don't be wastin' time then. Get on with it, will yuh?" he rasped stoically.

Brief planning ensued. The crusty partners allowed Russ to take charge, explaining the route he proposed taking. At last all was in readiness, their guns loaded and pockets weighed down with shells.

"We'll shove off now. Squeeze out a few shots, Dad," the young fellow directed. "And keep it up once in a while till you hear us cut loose."

Cobb nodded, his weathered face revealing mixed feelings of pride and rebellion at the cool instructions of his son. He turned his back on them. Before they slipped out the rear door his rifle was already pounding methodically.

"Make for the barn," Russ muttered tersely to his companions. They ran that way, making it and flattening themselves against the back while they waited. Apparently they had not been seen. Cobb pointed to the fringe of brush along the rising slope of the hills, and taking a deep breath he headed for it with long strides.

Crouching in the shelter of tumbled rocks, they congratulated themselves on getting away from the house undetected. Thick mesquite cluttered the rear edge of the bench, and by crawling or darting from clump to clump they rapidly covered a considerable distance. Dropping down off the far end of the bench through scattered rock patches, they reached a gullied wash that ran straggling out across the range.

"Thing to do is to work out past them and close in from behind," Russ muttered to the others.

Keeping a sharp watch, they traveled as fast as they could, running occasionally in the soft soil. The gunfire had slacked off, making it hard to determine the position of the renegades. The infrequent rifle shot, heard now and then, young Cobb believed to be his father.

This wash ran into a tangled network of other washes and gullies, leading them far out on the range. Thus far they had neither been detected or shot at, but it was hot, laborious work. At length Cobb pointed to a rocky ridge rising a couple of hundred feet above the surrounding range. "We can look right down on them from up there—"

Working their way upward, they soon reached the top. Guns ready, they crawled forward cautiously and peered over and down. The brushy swells and most of the protecting washes lay open to their gaze for a quarter of a mile in every direction. To their chagrin, no sign of life was anywhere to be seen.

"Blame it all, we stalled too long!" exclaimed Sam.

"We didn't," retorted Russ hotly. "It took a while to get here. If they got fed up and pulled out, that's just our luck."

"Anyhow, they're gone," said Ezra. "No harm done, and we was tryin' to break it up." Stepping into the open and exposing himself briefly to see whether he would draw fire, he made sure that the attackers had indeed drawn off. "Well, that's that. We'll climb down and tell old Ben he can breathe again."

[15]

Heading back toward Antler, Russ Cobb methodically sought out the point from which the attack had been directed at the ranch. He located scuffed boot tracks in a shallow wash, and also scattered through the brush. Discharged cartridge cases lay about. Finally he found where the renegades had hidden their horses, the prints of shod hoofs plain in the slanting late-afternoon sunshine.

"Three of 'em," Ezra ventured, studying their sign. "Them guns sounded like fifteen. Sure makes a man ask himself what they was after!"

"Maybe it does you." Young Cobb was curt. "I happen to know. They were after Dad's hide!"

Looking at him sidewise, Ezra wondered what anger and indignation would impel the Cobbs to do next. "You'll be able to prove that, I suppose—after yuh hit back?" he hazarded.

"With you two as witnesses?" countered Russ, snorting. "I won't leave it at that either. I'm going after my bronc, Ez, and I'll trace those buzzards wherever they went!"

Ezra nodded his approval. "I'll go with yuh, boy."

Ben Cobb was at first angry, and then disgusted, when they returned to the ranch with their story. "Be dang sure yuh find out where they went," he ordered sourly.

"I figure to," Russ answered briefly, not delaying for further talk. Picking up his bronc where he had hidden it in the brush, he found Ezra and Sam ready to accompany him. They set off hastily, returning to where they had found the tracks of the renegades.

Here Ezra took over. A tracker without peer on this range, he unraveled the scrambled sign while the others were wondering where to commence. "This way," he

125

called. They fell in a little to his rear, giving him plenty of room to work.

The trail led off across the range, clinging to low ground. It explained how the attackers had been able to slip away without detection. Following at first with ease, Ezra soon began to slow his pace.

"What's the trouble?" Russ asked sharply.

The big fellow shrugged. "Light ain't gettin' any better" he tossed back briefly. "For another thing, them birds got to thinking about exactly what we're doin'. They been tryin' to break trail!"

It was unexpected. Losing the sign, Ez picked it up again and followed it for another mile. Evening light was beginning to pale out by the time he lost the tracks for good. Although the tracker showed his disgust over this failure, Russ was not altogether disappointed.

Sam noted his abstraction. "What yuh thinkin' about, Cobb?" he asked. Russ waved a hand significantly.

"Remember what Dad said?" he demanded. "He swore it was Colcord who tried to smoke us out. We follow this trail—and where does it peter out? . . . Well onto Saw Buck range," he answered himself crisply. "And within a mile of Crip's place! What does that indicate to you?"

They eyed him blankly for a second. That it looked bad neither offered to deny. "Still it don't prove a blasted thing," Sam pointed out. "Maybe somebody wanted the signs to point straight to Colcord! We lost them hombres—and they could be restin' their feet in Ganado right now."

"Or in Colcord's house!" Cobb brought it out reluctantly, obliged by strict justice to express his thought.

"Well—" Ezra gathered himself together coolly. "There's one way to find that out in a hurry. We'll ride in on Colcord," he said. "And if he had a hand in that business I'd like to see him hide it from me!"

To his surprise Russ promptly shook his head. "No, I won't go there," he said flatly. "If Colcord is guilty, Jess Lawlor can handle it. . . . Only this morning Crip accused me of stealing his herd money," he added for their enlightenment. "Stevens and I trailed Gyp Carmer to Ganado and got it back for him—and this is the pay I get!" he ended bitterly.

Sam nodded thoughtfully. "I can see why yuh don't want any part of the place," he agreed. "But we ain't lettin' this drop. Me and Ez will ride in there and see what we can find out," he offered. "Is that what yuh want?"

Cobb hesitated. "I—don't know what to say, Sam," he confessed. "Colcord was dead wrong about me, and I'd hate to be just as wrong about him! But how *can* I be?" His taut tone revealed the struggle he was undergoing.

"Shucks." Ezra was gruff. "Right or wrong, we got a right to show ourselves at Saw Buck. It's gettin' dark anyway. We can't do nothin' here."

Russ reined back. "Yes, you'd better to on," he decided. "I won't go myself. Dad needs me. He may have a bad night with that shoulder."

"Sure—and if we learn anything we'll let yuh know," Sam promised.

They left it at that. Pushing on toward Saw Buck, the partners discussed the situation with greater freedom than they had allowed themselves in Cobb's presence. "I don't think Colcord had any hand in it at all," said Ezra sagely.

"Not if that girl knew it," seconded Sam. "She wouldn't go for no rough stuff—and where would Crip scare up his help, anyway?" he pursued. "We know there had to be three of 'em. Colcord *might* have been along; but Kip McKinley's too old and stove up for that stuff. And they must've been busy with that Lazy Mare stock too."

Dusk was thickening as they rode into the Saw Buck yard, still talking it over. Three men were talking near the corral. It gave Sam a jolt until he recognized Pat Stevens as one of them. The others were Colcord and his aging puncher.

"Well! I thought you boys were home by this time," was Pat's greeting.

"Come over here Stevens," Ezra said purposefully, halting at distance. "I want to talk to yuh."

Pat started forward, and Sam rode on to join the

rancher and McKinley, giving the pair a chance for a few words in private.

"What now, Ez?" asked Stevens calmly as they met.

Ez plunged into a terse account of the attack on Antler into which he and Sloan had blundered. "Young Russ got into it too," he wound up. "After them hombres pulled out we trailed 'em over here to Saw Buck."

"But you lost them then?"

Ezra nodded. "Wasn't no great surprise though. Old Ben raved about it had to be Colcord—and now Russ ain't so certain himself . . . He wouldn't ride on in with us."

"You mean Russ is out there on the range—?"

Ezra wouldn't vouch for that. "He *said* he'd shove along home. With Ben hit in the shoulder, he seemed a mite worried about him."

Breaking off abruptly, Pat turned to call over his shoulder. "Come here, Colcord," he said. "I want you to hear this."

Crip stumped out to join them, peering doubtfully at Ezra. "Yes—?"

"Tell him your story, Ez," Pat instructed.

Complying, the lanky tracker was careful to state the established facts only. Colcord listened with gathering uneasiness. "Yuh followed them lead-slingin' wolves over here?" he barked at the end. "And Russ Cobb came with yuh? Why didn't yuh bring him to me?"

"He says you didn't want him around only this mornin'," Ezra gave back bluntly.

"Why hang it! *He* knows he never laid a hand on my steer money—and I know it too now," protested Colcord. "Won't he give us no chance to explain—?"

"Explain what?" put in Sam shrewdly.

"Well—that we had nothin' to do with that shootin' over at Antler, for one thing," returned Crip. "Stevens knows it. . . ."

"I only know that I found you home half an hour ago," put in Pat strictly. Actually he had not the slightest belief that Saw Buck was involved. But it could do no harm for Colcord to marshal the proofs of his innocence.

"That's right, but—hang it, boy!" For an instant old Crip was confused. "I've been busy with that Lazy Mare beef all afternoon," he averred strongly. "We know who tried to make off with my money—and with you paid off, I'm sittin' on top of the heap. *I* got no reason for any such crazy caper!"

At that moment Penny called them to supper. "Is that Ezra—and Sam?" she said from the door. "Come in, all of you, while everything is hot."

They moved that way, still discussing the situation in heavy tones. "It's funny how hard it is to prove where yuh been at any particular time," complained Colcord fretfully. "But Kip knows we weren't anywhere near Antler—and here's Penny too," he added as they stepped in. "Tell Stevens what we were doin' all afternoon, girl!"

"I'm afraid we were congratulating ourselves on having got the best of you, Pat," she replied smilingly, not recognizing the gravity of the moment. "Dad has been simply gloating over those fat steers—"

"Never mind. You don't have to explain," Pat caught her up. In a few words he acquainted the girl with events on the Antler. "Old Ben is ranting about your father as usual," he explained. "But I know better. I've been trying to get out of Colcord what kind of an alibi he did have."

"I don't suppose he has any except my word for it," he said seriously. "And maybe Kip's." Already she was beginning to question the effect of the latest developments on Russ Cobb, her face clouded.

Pat waved her away. "Get that grub on the table, Penny. . . . I don't need to be told that your dad wouldn't know where to pick up three tough killers, even if he wanted to use them!"

It set an easier tone for the talk which followed. If Colcord showed considerable curiosity about who could be interested in assaulting the Cobbs, Pat was slow to answer. "Ben has grown mighty testy lately," he evaded. "We don't know what enemies he might have made."

For a time they were silent, busily eating. Penny was an excellent cook, and all did justice to her efforts. With appetites somewhat appeased, the talk started up again. "You never did tell us how yuh tracked down that money, Stevens," the rancher suggested. "Yuh followed young Cobb away from here, and that's all I do know."

Pat took full advantage of the opportunity to relate the events of the morning. Russ Cobb lost nothing in the narrative, and Penny's eyes were suspiciously bright at the end.

"Then it was Russ who discovered the money hidden in Carmer's hat?" she asked. "It's plain that we owe him fully as much as we owe you, Pat—"

He nodded ready agreement. "Probably you owe him more," he seconded generously. "It was him that remembered seeing that kid puncher prowling around over here, or we'd never have connected the man with this business."

Crip was following the tale with care. "What kind of a lookin' hombre is this Carmer, Stevens?" he queried.

"He's dark skinned, with dead black hair, narrow eyes, and kind of snaky looking," Pat supplied. "Skinny and sort of slouched over—in his early twenties, I judge."

"Why, I met that bird myself!" Colcord grew animated. "Cobb and I ran into him on our way home the other day. He was with that bunch that tried to rob me the first time!"

Penny had been spared the story of the assault on her father, though she had suspected something at the time. Though he bore the marks of conflict himself, Russ had not remained long enough at the ranch following her own arrival that day to answer her questions. Now she insisted on learning what had happened.

Colcord gave a spirited account of how the four roughs had waylaid Cobb and himself on the trail. With the event safely past, he was able to treat it with some humor. The girl did not find anything funny about it, however, her face sobering.

"Oh, Dad—that's just so much more we owe Russ," she got out swiftly. "He risked his life for you. How *could* you ever have considered him guilty of theft this morning, knowing that—?"

Kip McKinley, the gnarled puncher sitting at the lower end of the table, broke silence now with a dissenting growl. "That's where yuh got it all wrong, girl," he protested. "Your pop is no fool, nor I ain't either! Russ Cobb works for War Ax, same as them other birds, don't he? Naturally he put up a show of fightin'—even if he deliberately led Colcord into a trap. *He* wasn't aimin' to give hisself away so easy!"

The words gave rise to a burst of energetic protest or agreement from almost everyone at the table. Even Sam Sloan, who did not know young Cobb very well, at least pretended to be impressed by the plausibility of old Kip's reasoning.

But Penny refused to be talked down. "I'm thoroughly ashamed of you all," she exclaimed warmly. "You are still meanly suspicious, although Russ's every action proves him to be our friend! I never doubted him for a minute. What must he do to satisfy you?"

Pat winked at her, nodding his private approval. But old Crip chose to pretend umbrage. "What *are* yuh drivin' at, girl?" he roared. "By your talk I'll be tryin' next to land that boy in jail. No such thing! Would I be ridin' all over with him if I didn't trust him?"

He sprang up from the table awkwardly to lend emphasis to his retort. It was at this exact moment that one of the kitchen windows suddenly burst inward with a crash and jingle of shattering glass. In the act of uttering some even more emphatic statement, Colcord gave a gasping cry and throwing up his arms, fell headlong.

Startled as all were by the unwarned suddenness of it, Stevens was half on his feet before the musical tinkle of falling glass fragments had ceased. It was full dark now, unbroken blackness showing beyond the window frames. Busy with supper, Penny had thought nothing of her neglect to draw the curtains. It was Ezra who deftly jerked them closed in the first dragging moment of stunned silence.

"Father's been shot," the girl gasped. She was the first to break through her paralysis, dropping beside him. Pat and Sam were close at her elbow. One look told the story. Old Crip had been knocked senseless by the lethal slug. They saw the blood staining his gray hair as Penny cradled his lax head.

"Take it easy, girl," urged Pat swiftly, having a closer look. "That's not a fatal hit. From the looks, it grazed his head mighty close—"

"Hurry," she gave back tightly. "There's hot water on the stove—and clean cloths there in the chest."

For a wonder, old Kip was as agile on his feet as any in this emergency. He handed the girl a dampened cloth with which she stanched the ugly furrow creasing Colcord's head above the temple. For a minute or two all waited tensely, until the unconscious rancher stirred uneasily and uttered a groan.

"He's comin' around," jerked out Sam hopefully.

Pat nodded. "It was the shock that knocked him out," he gave his opinion. "He'll be okay in a few minutes."

"Why not lay him on the couch there," proposed Ezra. "Get hold of his legs, Sam, and we'll make him comfortable."

It was old McKinley who stalked the length of the kitchen and back while they were thus occupied, his deeply-lined face knotted with anger. "Now maybe you birds will believe what I say once in a while!" he jerked out abruptly.

Pat turned to look in his direction, but it was Penny who found something ominous in the exclamation. "Why do you say that, Kip?" she inquired steadily.

McKinley snorted. "Because I stopped hopin' and started stickin' to facts," he retorted briefly. "Who would it be that wants Colcord out of the way bad enough to do somethin' about it? And who are we sure had that chance tonight? . . . It was Russ Cobb that pulled that trick—don't care what any of yuh say!" he wound up harshly.

"Kip—please!" Penny stared at him aghast from where she knelt beside her father. "How can you even think such a thing?"

Kip continued to glower at her stubbornly. "Open up your eyes, girl! Cobb was out there with Sloan and Ezra just a while ago, wasn't he? He wouldn't come on in with 'em because he was waitin' for this chance! Think what yuh want; but I ain't blindin' myself about him, I tell yuh right straight!"

"You are wrong," denied Penny courageously. "Terribly wrong, Kip. I'm certain of it!"

"Am, eh? Just how'll yuh go about provin' that?" the angry puncher snarled.

The girl jumped to her feet swiftly. "I'll throw open the door and show myself. I'll draw that killer's fire." She returned his look undaunted. "That will prove it was not Russ. He would never fire at me!"

Before they realized that she meant what she said, she reached the door and flung it back, standing clearly silhouetted in the light from the lamps.

For a long breath no shot came. Nothing but dead silence answered her bold challenge from the night-blanketed range.

[16]

Penny's face twisted sharply as she stood there staring out into the gloom. "Go ahead and shoot, why don't you?" she cried.

Kip McKinley chuckled sourly as Ezra hastily drew her aside and thrust the door to. "Yuh said it right, girl," jeered the puncher cynically. "Russ Cobb would never shoot at you—and he didn't!"

Almost ready to burst into tears following the failure of her experiment, Penny put her hands over her face. It realized her genuine distress.

"Forget it, Penny. It doesn't mean a thing," he declared crisply, frowning at old Kip. "Let's not get jumpy about this," he urged. "Whoever took a shot at Colcord wouldn't be likely to stick around waiting to see what happened next. He didn't let fly at you because he was already gone over the hill."

She took comfort from this, but her face remained sad. "You're right of course. But it's terrible that Russ or anyone else should have to answer to such accusations."

Breaking off, she gave her attention once more to her father. The discussion of who could have fired the treacherous shot did not cease at once, McKinley arguing stubbornly for his views. Old and set in his ways, he would probably never accord the Cobbs credit for anything. But Penny had ceased to listen.

"How is he now?" asked Pat, moving close for a look at the rancher.

Colcord surprised him by endeavoring to sit up. The girl sought to force him back but he would have none of it, struggling to an upright position on the couch. "Some skunk is after my skin and no mistake," he got out forcibly.

"You were lucky, Colcord," Pat told him. "That slug barely broke the skin. If you hadn't been moving at the time, the chances are you never would again."

Crip grunted, moving his head about and wincing. The bandage with which Penny had covered his wound gave him a piratical appearance, augmented just now by the ferocity of his expression. "Dang nuisance if a man ain't safe in his own house!" Gathering strength swiftly he ground out the exclamation with gusto. "I don't suppose yuh saw who done that—?"

"We didn't have t' see—" began Kip promptly.

But Ezra had had enough of the old fellow's crusty dogmatism. "Shut up, McKinley," he cut the other off disgustedly. "You don't know nothin', and we don't. Let's tell the simple truth for once!"

"Kip has accused Russ of trying to kill you," Penny explained candidly. "But I refuse to believe it, Dad."

Crip nodded, glancing from one to another dubiously. "Funny though, how Sam and Ez remembered leaving him out there on the range when they came," he began half-ashamed of his own thought.

"We didn't," Ezra contradicted with spirit. "Told yuh

ie wouldn't come in with us and headed back home,
iidn't I? That was the best part of an hour ago—"

The obvious retort, that Cobb might easily have turned
ind come back unseen, was voiced by no one. That it
iccurred to old Kip at least was plain from the rebel-
ion in his wrinkled face. Penny caught it.

"I'm ashamed of you all!" she burst out sharply.
Again and again Russ Cobb has come to our aid when
ie received no credit whatever for his actions! Why
iust you insist on blaming him, without true cause, for
verything that happens?"

Sobered by his experience, Colcord was both temperate
ind deliberate. "I don't expect yuh really tried to find out
vho it was out there," he broke the heavy silence shrewd-
/.

Sam started guiltily, but it was his lanky partner who
ame up with the logical answer. "We can make sure if
e's gone," he said gruffly. "Don't see how yuh could
ll who it was or wasn't, till daylight."

"Maybe there's one way," put in Pat quietly. "But I
e you two are itching to get out there right now. Go
iead, and make sure nobody's prowling around first—"

They needed no more. "Please be careful," the girl
rged as they made for the back door. Slipping out, they
on reached the covering sage and circled cautiously.
he angle from which Colcord was shot had given them
e general direction. A faint glow from the curtained
indows enabled them to judge their distance from the
iuse.

No sign of life remained anywhere in the area they
arched, only the sage clumps rustling softly in the er-
tic night wind.

"Stevens said it the first time," Ezra gave his opinion
last. "He's long gone, whoever it was. Ain't nothin'
r us here. Let's not scuff out his tracks."

They made their way back to the ranch house. All
es turned toward them as they entered the kitchen.
m shook his head. "Not a thing out yonder," he an-
unced. "What was it yuh was figurin' to spill, Stevens?"

Pat delayed a moment. "I hesitate to suggest this," he

acknowledged. "But I've never yet lost ground by going straight to the heart of things. How would it be," he proposed, watching their reactions, "if we all shove over there to Antler right now and put this up to the Cobbs?"

"Unh-uh!" Kip McKinley was the first to veto any such project without hesitation. "Not me." But the others were more receptive. Even Penny looked hopeful.

"It's foolish, of course. But I'm sure that a sensible talk with them would persuade you all they had nothing to do with this treacherous attack," she said. "I'm perfectly willing to try, Pat. But—I don't know whether Father should try to make it or not—"

It was exactly the right remark to cause Colcord to bristle indignantly. "Why shouldn't I make it?" he fired out. "I'd like t' see somebody try to prevent me from goin' along!"

Pat could not help asking himself whether the old firebrand had not had enough excitement for one night. "I might be smart for you to stay put and rest, at that," he suggested mildly. "You know how Ben Cobb flies off the handle at the sight of you."

"He'll have to get over it," declared Colcord stiffly. "I don't aim to go on duckin' him for the rest of my days and he might as well know it!"

"But Dad—riding a horse while you're in your present condition will be very uncomfortable," pleaded Penny.

"Shucks. Hitch up the wagon then," retorted her parent hardily. "Yuh ain't leavin' me here, an' that's final."

Nodding his assent, Pat thought that if it was barely possible to effect a reconciliation between these hard headed and stiff-necked neighbors it was certainly worth the effort. Not old Kip, however. Trying to argue his employer out of an attempt which he believed to be pure folly, he stubbornly refused to hitch up the rig.

"I don't want any part of sendin' yuh over to Antler to get finished off for good," the puncher averred vehemently.

Laughing him to scorn without making any impression whatever, Ezra and Sam got the ranch wagon ready. Trying his legs, Colcord pronounced himself eager for the start. The party gathered in the yard, all intending to go except Kip.

"We'll leave yuh here to look after things," the rancher told him tolerantly. "Just keep an eye peeled, Kip. We'll probably be back in short order."

Kip grumbled something or other decidedly uncomplimentary to their hopes. No one paid him any heed. Getting Colcord settled in the wagon, they set off. It was a dark night and the moon would not be up till later. Fortunately it was only a matter of two or three miles to Antler, and the trail was fairly plain. A dim light gleamed in Cobb's house as they came up on the bench, but there was no other sign of life.

"Try the door, Sam," said Pat quietly.

Sloan dismounted and banged on the door, calling out, "Are yuh there, Cobb? It's Sam Sloan again!"

Several minutes passed before there was any response. Then old Ben could be heard moving about inside. The light went out, and he called through the door in muffled tones.

"Who is it again? . . . You, Sloan?" Still he did not offer to unbar and open up. "Who's with you?"

"Come on, let me in, will yuh?" Sam exclaimed impatiently. "There ain't a thing to worry about, Ben!"

They heard the bar being lifted down, and the door creaked open cautiously. "What in creation yuh after at this hour?" came Cobb's gruff demand.

"Light a light, for gosh sake," ordered Sam. "This ain't another raid, whatever you think! Loosen up, oldtimer. I want to talk to you and Russ."

Cobb thumped around, getting a coal-oil lantern lit and then a second. He may have overheard sounds of activity from the yard, but his eyes flared up and then hardened when he looked around to find Pat Stevens, Penny Colcord and her father standing in the door behind Sam. Ezra was not far away.

"Well! What's the meanin' of this?" was all he could manage, slowly backing away a step or two.

"We dropped over to iron out our differences, Cobb,"

began Colcord cheerfully. He started to step in, then paused. "Are we welcome here or not?"

Ben neglected to answer, turning his head as Pat spoke up. "Things have happened today that make some sort of an understanding advisable," Stevens stated, entering and standing quietly in the lantern light. "Is Russ home, Cobb?"

"Reckon he is—" Ben was still glowering at them sullenly, striving to swallow his indignation.

"Could you get him? He ought to be in this," Pat insisted firmly.

Without response, Cobb moved to the foot of a rough stairway leading upward into shadowy darkness, and called harshly. "Russ! Are yuh awake? . . . . Come down here, boy."

After a delay boots clumped, and still later Russ Cobb came thumping down the steps, his hair tousled and with sleep in his eyes. They jerked wide at the first glimpse of Penny and her father.

"Well, this is sure unexpected!" He tried to straighten up and smooth his hair down somewhat. "What *is* that bandage under your hat, Colcord?"

"That's proof that a man ain't safe in his own house on this range," answered Crip gruffly. "I got it after dark tonight, while I was eatin' supper!"

Ben Cobb moved forward, bristling. "Sure of that, are yuh?" he rasped offensively. "It couldn't have been during the afternoon, by any chance—"

"No, you're wrong there," inserted Pat quickly. "It happened while I was in his house, Cobb. I saw it."

Ben only grunted. He had pulled on a shirt before opening the door, but it was indifferently buttoned. As he leaned forward, thrusting his jaw towad them, the shirt sagged aside and they saw the stained bandage covering his own side and shoulder.

"Picked up some lead yourself, eh?" growled Crip, pausing to stare.

"I'm still wonderin' if I didn't get it about the same time you did," retorted Cobb thinly, jerking his chin down.

"Easy now, old man." Pat thought it time to make a

few things plainly understood. "I certainly don't blame you for being suspicious after what's happened. Sam and Ezra told me about the attack on your place here. I was at Saw Buck too early for either Colcord or Kip McKinley to have gotten back home if they'd been mixed up in that deal. And I *was* sitting across the table from Colcord when a slug came through the window and knocked him cold."

Ben frowned at him coldly. "So yuh hotfooted it over here to find out if we done it," he hazarded.

"Well, did yuh?" challenged Colcord before Pat had a chance to cut him off.

"No! I only wish I'd thought of it!" Ben thundered uncompromisingly. "So now yuh know, yuh can haul your traps out of here, kit and kaboodle!"

The young people listened to this fiery exchange without speaking, distress and dismay in their faces. Penny spoke up now, voicing her earnest desire for mutual understanding. "Mr. Cobb, we heard what happened to you today," she said quickly. "It's to assure you we've been busy all afternoon with new stock that we came here tonight. Russ knows this is true—"

"Dad knows it too," put in Russ briefly, hoping by reminding Ben of the range-firing episode to awaken his conscience while accusations were being bandied about.

"I know you're pretty cocky these days," Cobb hurled at Colcord incorrigibly. "You'll be needin' more range soon, won't yuh?"

Crip snorted. "You're still rememberin' that phony range-grass affair," he charged. "Where *did* yuh get that idea, Cobb—if a man can have a straight answer?"

Pat was himself interested in what the reply would be, having witnessed the clash to which it had given rise. Old Ben looked briefly confused, recalling his flat statement that Russ had witnessed the attempt to steal his grass.

"Since yuh got your beef back off my range in a hurry, we'll say no more about it," he evaded.

Crip Colcord looked at Stevens expressively. "So much for your fine scheme, boy," he growled.

"Look, Cobb," Pat said patiently, turning to Ben. "We'd really like to know where you got that story about Saw Buck stock being on your grass. If it isn't too much trouble?"

Ben made a violent gesture. "All right! I seen it with my own eyes, if yuh got to know," he snarled.

"*You* saw it?" All stared at him, surprised. "And will you swear you saw Kip McKinley with the stock?" thrust on Pat quickly.

Cobb stalled. "Come on, now. Who else could it've been?" he retorted defensively.

"But you didn't see McKinley to recognize him without any possible mistake?" Stevens appeared determined to force the man to a straight answer.

"Didn't have to, I tell yuh! Hang it all—" Cornered, Cobb could only take refuge in vehement protestation.

"Hold it right there." Pat was firm. "We'll go along with your story that Colcord's beef *could* have been over your line. But the whole point is, Cobb—*who did it?*"

"Well, now," old Crip broke in, missing Pat's object altogether. "I ain't prepared to go that far, Stevens! Ben's been lookin' for an excuse to jump me. This wild yarn is what he picked!"

Cobb stalked forward to glare at him wickedly. "That's a lie!" he flashed. "I know you're after my range, Colcord! You thought you'd grab Pack Traver's spread after my own son cleared the way—only it didn't work! So now you're tryin' to crowd me out!"

To anyone less deeply entangled than himself, it was so obviously preposterous a charge that Colcord was up in arms in a twinkling. "Take that back, yuh schemin' old spider," he roared, his beard bristling truculently. The stinging words would have precluded any possibility of compliance, even if old Ben had been so inclined. His answer was prompt and unmistakable. Hauling his good arm back, he smote Colcord violently across the face.

Crip staggered, but he was game. Catching his balance, he hurled himself forward, fists flailing. For a moment the two old warriors buffeted each other soundly, their breath rasping. It came so suddenly that during a space of paralyzing surprise no one made a move to halt it. Then Russ sprang forward. Instinctively protecting his father as he crowded in between the two, he gave Colcord a thrust that almost sent him headlong to the floor. Ezra caught the tottering rancher in time to save him a nasty fall.

"Russ, be careful!" Penny's voice was unconsciously sharp.

Making sure that old Ben was subdued, the young fellow turned to her slowly. "Seems to me it's time for somebody else to be a little careful," he brought out dangerously.

"What do you mean?" she caught him up coolly. "There was no reason for Mr. Cobb to strike Dad——"

"And what was the reason for Colcord coming over here at all?" he threw at her fiercely. "You came over to browbeat us. Dad knows that, and I know it! Just because you've got Pat Stevens and his friends to back you up, it don't mean you can bully us into a thing. You might as well know it!"

"How can you say that?" she gasped, her pink face slowly draining white.

"I can say more," exclaimed Russ forcefully. "You all had plenty to say, I notice! But every word that comes out of Pop's mouth is a lie—according to you!"

"But I said nothing! We only tried to say——" she began miserably, realizing more quickly than he how hopeless all this wrangling was.

"You're trying to say everything that happens to us is a pipe dream!" flared Russ condemningly. "I never saw your stock on our grass—I'll admit that. I didn't see Colcord or McKinley or any of you over here this afternoon when somebody tried to wipe us out. But I'll still believe Dad before I listen to you! And what's more, it'll always be that way!"

Penny stared at him with wide eyes. All hope and animation seemed to have deserted her tragic face. She turned blindly and stumbled toward the door. "Come, Dad," she choked.

Pat Stevens was the last to give up, standing by the door and surveying the Cobbs doubtfully. "I know it's hard for anyone to use his best judgment when tempers are loose," he said quietly. "But I still don't believe you and Colcord have any real quarrel, Cobb. I hope you'll change your mind about this when you've thought it over."

"Pah!" Old Ben was bitterly defiant. "When the old buzzard stops tryin' to make me believe black is white, maybe I'll listen," he shot out vindictively.

Pat knew it was useless to hope to move him in his present mood. He looked briefly at the younger man. "Don't take this too serious, Russ," he advised. "We all say things we're sorry for, one time or another."

"Did you hear me say I was sorry?" The young fellow's forced bluster, more than his closed face, indicated that he was already inwardly regretting his vehemence.

Pat shrugged. "I'm satisfied you've both got the Colcords sized up wrong," was his final word as he turned to leave. "If anything turns up to change this unfortunate situation I'll let you know."

Rejoining the others in the yard, he found Colcord being helped into the rig. Penny had already climbed to the seat and was straightening out the reins. Sam and Ezra swung into the saddle, and once Stevens was mounted the little party set off.

No word was said until Antler lay far behind. At last Colcord squared around in his seat to accost Pat, riding at the wagonside. "Lot of good this trip did!" he growled in indignation. "I been tryin' to make yuh see how unreasonable Cobb is. Things are worse off now than they was before!"

"Maybe not altogether." Pat had to use care in getting across the point he wanted to make. "For instance, there's no question that Russ was in bed asleep when we got there—"

"No one ever really questioned that, Pat," rejoined Penny promptly. Even in her hurt displeasure she was determined to do the puncher justice. "To believe that Russ shot Dad, even if Kip says so, is surely wrongheaded."

"Don't be too sure about that," the level-eyed man demurred firmly. "You'll freely admit, Penny, that the air is full of wild suspicions right now. Our whole trouble is that while we don't *want* to believe these things, we lack convincing proof one way or another."

"Now you're talkin', boy," inserted Sam gruffly. "Some of us know one thing or another, but not enough to add together. Danged if it don't look like a put-up job!"

"Put up by who?" rasped Crip with unexpected vigor, not yet ready to remove the chip from his shoulder.

"That's exactly what we're trying to find out," Pat squelched him coolly.

"So how'll yuh do that?"

"By pinning it on the right man, of course," supplied Pat. But it was Ezra who relieved the tension by laughing gruffly.

"That's exactly what's got us stumped," he pointed out dryly. "Colcord and old Cobb have been findin' out that yuh can't settle it by arguin'."

There was more talk, but as Ezra suggested it led to nothing. Twenty minutes later they drew near to Saw Buck. Sam sang out warningly as they entered the yard. "It's us, McKinley! We're back," he called. "Where are yuh?"

The single lamp left burning in the ranch house kitchen was still lit, but it failed to reveal old Kip hustling out to greet them. Penny brought the rig to a stand, for a moment not knowing what to think.

"Ain't shoved off to bed, has he?" Ezra speculated curiously. "We've all had a rough day—"

"No." Colcord stoutly refuted this. "McKinley was left

on guard here—and whatever yuh say, he never slacked a chore like that."

"Maybe he heard somethin' out on the range and went to investigate," hazarded Sam, trying to look about. At this late hour the moon was just breaking over the horizon, throwing a faint glow over their surroundings which would presently brighten.

"That's possible." Pat was practical. "Put the rig away for Colcord, will you, Sam? And then see if Kip's pony is gone from the corral, while we look the house over."

Reaching the ground with Penny's help, Crip stumped to the door. Pat was close behind the pair as they stepped in. The kitchen, they saw at once, was empty. It occurred to Penny, however, that McKinley might have suffered one of his mild digestive attacks, which now and then obliged the old fellow to lie down for a time. Lighting another lamp, the girl moved into the other rooms while the men waited. She came back after a delay, shaking her head with a worried look.

"I can't find Kip, and he isn't in his room," she said.

Sam came running at the moment, to thrust in through the door. "McKinley's bronc is out there," he announced. "Did yuh find him here?"

The blank looks on their faces gave him his answer. "Hang it! Where is he, then?" the little man complained, perplexed by so complete a disappearance as this.

"He must be around somewhere," Pat caught him up. "We'll scatter around outside and have a look—"

With one accord they turned back into the yard. Rapidly strengthening now, the moon threw its pale illumination over the brush; but it was barely above the skyline as yet, and cast black shadows here and there about the house. Having already started his search, Ezra was to be seen working in slowly widening circles through the deep patches of gloom.

It was he who cried out abruptly before the others had barely commenced to hunt. "Here yuh are! Over here," called Ez. He stood waiting while they hurried forward.

Pat was the first to reach his side, with Penny close

behind. Sam came waddling up hastily, and Colcord puffed forward to lean over and peer sharply into the deep shadow under a sage clump.

"*That* ain't Kip—layin' out here?" the rancher barked incredulously.

Bending down, for answer Ezra scratched a match on his thigh and held it up. Its brief flare revealed McKinley lying half on his face, one leg drawn up under him. Plainly to be seen in the middle of his back was a dark, spreading stain which marked where he had been ruthlessly shot.

"Him, alright." Ezra was curt. "I almost missed him, pushin' through this brush."

"Let's get him to the house," Pat interrupted. "There may be something we can do for him—"

Aged and spare as he was, the unfortunate puncher proved surprisingly light. Without a word, as they picked him up, Penny flew ahead to prepare for his arrival. So efficient was she that fresh sheets were spread on a downstairs cot and she was heating water by the time they crowded in through the kitchen door with their burden.

McKinley was deposited on the cot and Pat set about examining him. "Heart's awful weak, but he's still breathing," he announced. "Help me get his clothes off, Ez—"

They got Kip between the blankets, and Penny helped to clean his wound and bind him up. The slug had driven straight through the puncher's slight body, leaving a clean passage. Pat stood up at last, shaking his head.

"It's a matter of stamina. We've done all we can till a doctor gets here tomorrow," he said. "A lot depends on just how bad that bullet chewed him up inside." He looked down at the unconscious man soberly. "He may tough this out—or he could go out like a light."

They exchanged looks of mute uneasiness, and Colcord gave a fervent exclamation. "First me, and now Kip! By grab, Stevens," he burst out savagely. "This is the last straw!"

It seemed so. But Pat was earnestly pondering the occurrence, his brows furrowed. "What could have happened, exactly?" he asked musingly. "Either someone lured Kip out into the yard by a trick, or else he thought he was escaping something—"

"He was runnin' when they got him," put in Ezra unexpectedly.

"Made sure of that, did you?"

The lanky tracker nodded. "Near as yuh could see, he was alone out there though. Daylight might tell another story, o' course. But I didn't find no tracks, only his."

Colcord was moving restlessly about, his face gloomy. "There ain't a chance that young Cobb rushed over here ahead of us and done this?" he ground out, turning to gauge their reaction.

Pat broke from his abstraction wearing a faint frown. "You belong in bed, Colcord," he said bluntly. "You're not over that clip on the head, whatever you think. Come along, now. In the morning maybe we'll be able to look at this differently."

"Pat's right, Dad." Taking firm charge of her father, Penny would listen to no protest, leading him from the room. "You are overdoing it, and you know you . . . " The rest of her words were lost as the pair passed out of sight.

Pat and the Bar ES partners were left standing in the lamplight, lines of concentration marking the face of each. "What d' you say about this, boy?" inquired Ezra in the returned silence.

Pat made a brief gesture. "It's not all loss," he averred quietly. "I've been wrong before. But I think I see a light, Ez. From here out I'm going to work along those lines anyway."

"Let us in on it, Stevens." Sam was watching him closely.

"No—" The younger man was deliberate. "The trouble so far has been too much misdirected talk. Sorry, boys, but there's nothing personal meant. If you don't know, a chance word can't spill a thing. I'll hand this to the persons directly concerned," he proceeded evenly. "If it works you'll soon know plenty about it."

The crusty rawhides grumbled audibly over his parsimony. But they knew from experience that he would reveal nothing until he was ready. "I suppose you'll be takin' off somewheres by yourself?" growled Sam.

"No, we'll stay put right here tonight." Pat cheerfully ignored his sour temper. "I want you to go for the doctor in the morning, Sam. Old Kip may surprise us all. Ezra can stay here and guard the place for the day."

"Tryin' to get *me* knocked off, are yuh?" snarled the one-eyed man. But he had the grace to display a twisted grin. "Just wish some misguided pup would try it!"

The pair put up in the barn, while Pat took advantage of McKinley's unused room. Penny stayed up most of the night with the wounded man. In the early dawn she reported wearily that he had tossed and moaned considerably. "But Dad rested."

She got breakfast ready while Pat aroused the grumpy partners. They ate together. Afterward Pat saw Sam started off for the medico, and proceeded to get up his own bronc.

Ez watched him suspiciously. "Takin' me with yuh, Stevens?" he demanded.

Pat only smiled. "I've got a small chore of my own, Ez," he replied. "I'll probably be back before noon."

Making no attempt to conceal the fact that Antler was once more his objective, he set off. There was little activity to be observed about the Cobb ranch as he approached half an hour later. But smoke curled up from the stone and plaster chimney. Dismounting, Pat moved to the slab door. The treacherous attack of yesterday had left its mark on this side of the house. Pat was briefly examining the logs torn by slugs, before knocking, when the door was yanked open abruptly. Ben Cobb peered out, scowling when he saw who it was.

"You again, eh? Thought I heard somethin' out here."

Pat nodded, coolly pushing in. "Maybe I should have come over alone last night, Cobb. I thought of it this time. I've got something to tell you."

Young Russ was pulling on his shirt, getting ready for the day's work. Obviously he did not welcome Pat's appearance, hardly deigning to glance at him. Ben had prepared a scanty meal and it was waiting on the table.

"Go ahead. Don't let me hold up your breakfast," grunted Pat. "I've had mine."

But the rancher stood unmoving, regarding him with a frown, as if deciding how to dispose of his case. "Look, Stevens. Yuh seem to mean well," he rumbled. "Them friends of yours backed me up, and I ain't forgettin' in a hurry. But there ain't a thing you can say that'll mean anything. Why don't yuh just forget it?"

"Wait a minute. If this don't mean a thing to you," retorted Pat good-humoredly, "you're being bull-headed, Cobb. . . . You'll grant that Saw Buck was over here last night, lock, stock and barrel, I expect?"

"All but that tricky McKinley hombre," returned Ben promptly, sure he had caught Pat in an omission. *"He* knows better!"

"That's exactly the point. We left Kip to watch the place," Pat drove home, "while we were all over here together. And, Cobb—when we got back to Saw Buck we found McKinley shot through the back!"

"Good," rasped Cobb unfeelingly. "He won't be pesterin' me no more for a while!"

"But don't you get it?" exclaimed Pat. "Think a minute, man. Even Colcord knows neither of you had anything to do with that!"

Ben was savagely contemptuous. *"He* knows it, does he? So do we, Stevens! I could've told yuh that much before it happened."

Though he had been refusing flatly to listen, Russ began taking it all in alertly. Pausing with his coffee cup halfway to his mouth, he set it down again. "Go on, Stevens," he brought out tentatively. "What are you trying to say—?"

"Look at it yourself." Pat spread his hands. "To me it's proof in full that somebody's interested in setting you and Colcord at each other's throats."

"Bah. More talk—" began old Ben instantly. But Russ interrupted him with unaccustomed authority.

"Hold on, Dad. There's something to this. If the argument is between Saw Buck and ourselves, who else *is* doing all this wild shooting? And why?" Russ was reasonably sure he had long since guessed the answer, but he had despaired of ever driving it home to old Ben until Stevens came up with this single eloquent fact.

Forced to listen, his father was plainly annoyed: "Well, Colcord's doin' pretty good now, from all I hear. Maybe he's hired a few gunslingers and the deal backfired." It sounded hollow even to himself.

Russ stared at him scornfully. "You know better than that!"

"Who is it then?" Backed into a corner at last, Cobb glowered.

"Look around you," Pat suggested shrewdly. "Just who *would* be most pleased to see you two fighting?"

"Chuck Stober is my guess—and the only one I need," spoke up Russ boldly. "For that matter, Dad, I've seen it coming—"

"War Ax . . . ?" Ben Cobb looked astonished, if only briefly. "What claptrap is this? Next you'll be tellin' me it's Sheriff Lawlor!" he blurted sarcastically.

"Look at it again," Pat invited. "Who benefited from your trouble with Pack Traver? Was it Colcord—or you?" He paused significantly. "It was Chuck Stober, and nobody else!"

"Well—" Old Ben scratched his head, impressed in spite of himself. He found no convincing rebuttal to offer.

"I'll tell you something else," Russ rushed on, determined to clinch the argument. He related in detail how Stevens and Jess Lawlor had forced Stober to make restitution to Colcord following the stampede, and how two separate attempts had been made afterward by War Ax hands to relieve Crip of his money.

"I threw that to Stober myself," Russ confessed. "I didn't dare rub it in too hard for fear I might set him loose at you. Like a fool, I never guessed he was already at it!" he wound up self-condemningly. "Why else would he have been so easy on me?"

Ben heard him out with growing exasperation. He

stamped away from the table, only to turn and come back as if irresistibly drawn. "Maybe it is Stober!" he burst out harshly. "Where does that get yuh? We'll never be able to tear him down!"

It seemed so sound a statement of their position that Russ looked at Pat uneasily. The cool-eyed man was at no loss for a response.

"Don't be too sure of that, Cobb. I've found it helps a lot to know what you're up against. Stop fighting your head," he advised evenly, "and you may surprise even yourself. Does that add up?"

Persuaded despite himself by this hardheaded analysis, Ben only grunted. Pat would not leave it at that. "Can I have your promise to lay off of Colcord till we can take Stober's measure?" he demanded bluntly.

Delaying only briefly, Cobb gave his reluctant assent.

[18]

The doctor was at Saw Buck when Stevens returned following his visit to the Cobbs. Though he was well satisfied with his progress thus far, Pat put his own interests aside in his concern for Kip McKinley's condition.

"How is he?" he asked at once, when Penny met him at the kitchen door.

"Dr. Burch hasn't said," the girl replied, stepping out to join him in the yard. "But I'm afraid, Pat. Kip's age is against him, for one thing. He came to for a while, but is unconscious again now. He couldn't talk. The doctor is still working on him."

Pat shook his head. "This can't go on," he declared. "If Stober is responsible for still another death—and who else could it possibly be—something will have to be done."

It was said largely for Colcord's benefit as the rancher

stumped forward to join them. "What's that again?" growled Crip, catching a part of the ominous words.

Pat turned to him. "I pointed out to Cobb this morning that McKinley was shot while we were all over there together. You see what that spells," he said quietly.

Colcord peered at him sharply for a moment, and his jaws snapped shut. "By gum! That's right. I been so worried about old Kip, Stevens, that I never thought of it that way," he confessed. "It sure does look as if somebody's determined to keep Ben and me clawin' at each other—only this time he slipped!"

Pat was pleased that he was shrewd enough to see it for himself. "Now ask yourself who that would be," the younger man urged.

Crip looked puzzled for a minute, then scowled. "Search me," he grunted. "What's your guess?"

"It's no guess, Colcord." Pat was firm. "Circumstances point straight at Chuck Stober."

"What?" barked the rancher. He sounded as incredulous as Ben Cobb had been on first being told. "I don't believe it! Whatever gave yuh that idea, boy?"

Using many of the same arguments that had persuaded Cobb, Stevens called attention to the fact that it was Stober who had benefited from Pack Traver's death. "Don't forget it was his stock that stampeded across your range," he reminded curtly. "He didn't make good with that troublesome check for love of you, either—and both times an attempt was made to rob you, if it's escaped your attention, it was done by War Ax hands. In my opinion," he wound up, "Stober is trying his damnedest to ruin you and grab Saw Buck, much the same as he did with T Square!"

"No, you must have it all wrong somehow. Why pshaw, Stevens! Stober would never do a thing like this." Colcord waggled his beard stubbornly. "For that matter, he's had a friendly standin' offer up for Saw Buck for the past two years."

Pat was not surprised. "Long enough for him to decide to do something about it himself," he commented.

"No, I tell yuh he ain't that kind," Crip argued hardily. "I've known him too long—right up to now he's always been fair with me. He used to stop in and say howdy once in a while. I guess he's got busy lately—"

It was plain the wily War Ax owner had gone out of his way to impress his victim. A departure from Stober's usual tactics, it was the most insidious form of treachery.

"Then maybe you can explain this." Recounting his early visit to War Ax in search of Russ Cobb, Pat told how he had been slugged and bound and tossed into the grain shed. "Remember, Colcord, this happened to me personally—by Stober's order," he said flatly. "No matter what you say, he's friendly as a bear trap, and about as soft!"

Visibly shaken, Colcord tried weakly to summon up a last defense. He was opening his mouth to speak when a step sounded at the door and the doctor appeared. All turned to look at him.

Heavy-set and paunchy, Burch was an outspoken veteran noted alike for competence and bluntness. Stripped to his shirtsleeves now, the cuffs turned back, his uncompromising look was portentous.

"Is Kip better, Doctor?" inquired Penny anxiously.

Burch shook a short negative. "No."

"Do you mean—"

The medico jerked a nod. "He's gone. Chest smashed —one lung punctured. May have grazed his heart." He was pulling his sleeves down, laconic as ever. "Get my rig ready."

Sam, who was just coming forward, heard him and turned back to comply. Colcord emerged from the house a few minutes later, after a last look at his luckless employee, just as Dr. Burch made ready to depart. Sloan held the frisky sorrel team till the latter was settled in the seat; then he stepped nimbly aside. Not till they had watched the doctor roll out of the yard did Sam turn to Pat.

"McKinley's got a sister in Ganado, Stevens—he was tellin' me about her the other day. She'll probably want to claim the body. She's a spinster," he announced. "Shall I hitch up the flatbed?"

Pat glanced toward Colcord, who nodded heavily. "Tell Myra Kip's to be buried at my expense, Sam," he directed. "And find out when she wants the funeral. Me and Penny will try to be there."

Gloom held them all during the sad task of depositing McKinley's remains in the ranch wagon, decently covered. Ezra elected to accompany his pudgy partner, promising to return as soon as possible.

With their departure a heavy silence settled over Saw Buck. Well aware that his troubles were only increased, Colcord stumped back and forth in the yard, the lines of his face more deeply etched than ever. Pat prudently waited for him to come to a decision, while Penny simply waited.

Crip wheeled impatiently at last, hobbling toward them. "So maybe it is Stober's doing, Stevens! We'll never be able to nail him at his crooked work," he burst out, unconsciously echoing Ben Cobb's argument.

Pat knew that in this precise objection lay Colcord's real dread of the truth. He was prepared for it. "I never proposed taking any such charge to Jess Lawlor," he countered. "It's the last thing I would do, in fact."

"Then what good does it do if we know?" blurted Crip, too rattled for the moment to exercise sound judgment.

"Couldn't a—trap of some kind be set for the man?" put in Penny uncertainly.

Colcord looked up at once. "Why not? It's what he's been usin' on us!" His tone grew firmer. "We'll have to be smart though, to figure out somethin' that'll work on him—"

Pat's nod was thoughtful. "I've been turning it over," he allowed. "No scheme will be foolproof, of course. And the first try will have to work—or he'll be tipped off." He glanced up speculatively. "A lot depends on just how far you and Cobb are willing to work together."

Colcord snorted. "Are yuh askin' me that, or Ben?" he retorted.

Pat forced a wry grin. "I haven't overlooked that angle. And it'll have to be considered," he conceded.

Glancing about, he lowered his voice. "My plan, Colcord, would be for you to pretend to go into partnership with Cobb," he explained, "and start throwing up a fence between yourselves and War Ax. I'll almost guarantee that Stober will show his hand quick!"

Crip groaned. "I was afraid of somethin' like that. . . . But if I pass up any chance, it won't be playin' fair with Kip." He took a turn away from them, struggling with himself. "All right, Stevens." He swung back decisively. "If yuh can sell Cobb on any such crazy scheme, I'll play along. But only as far as I have to, to get results!"

"Dad, I knew you would!" exclaimed Penny, hope and courage ringing in her voice. "Perhaps even . . . Russ will change his mind when he hears."

For once her father was more cautious. "That remains to be seen," he qualified grimly. "You better talk, and talk fast, Stevens, when you go over there!"

Pat had concluded as much. He did not make the mistake of returning to Antler at once, giving old Cobb time to digest this morning's news before hammering it home with the announcement of McKinley's death.

Ezra appeared soon after midday, informing them that Kip's sister was handling the arrangements for his burial, and that Sloan had remained to help her. Interment would probably be on Thursday. Pat acquainted the Colcords with this information.

"I suppose you saw to it that word got back to Sheriff Lawlor?" he asked the lanky tracker.

Ez had. "He'll be out here t' nose around and ask questions about tomorrow."

Colcord looked dubious. "Will that—?" he began.

Pat shook his head quickly. "No. We'll tell Jess what we know and saw, and let him work on it."

It was all he said on the matter. Impatient as he was to head for Antler, he waited till late afternoon to make reasonably sure of finding Russ home when he got there. So close did he figure that when he arrived at the Cobb ranch he found the young fellow in the act of unsaddling.

"It must have crossed your mind a dozen times to quit War Ax," Pat opened up. "What about that?"

Russ glanced around darkly. "That's coming. But at my convenience, Stevens," he promised tersely. "If you know what I mean!"

Pat assented. "It means walking a tightrope, I imagine, but you'll have to manage. Pop home?"

Cobb swung around, straightening. "No, he's not. Hang it, Stevens—!" He corrected himself quickly. "You've got me jumpy, I guess, with all this shootin' going on. He must be out working the range somewhere." But his glance was worried.

Old Ben jogged into the yard while they were talking, dogmatic and unemotional as ever. "Gettin' so we see quite a lot of you, Stevens," he grumbled, not very pleased.

Pat ignored this, waiting till he put his horse up. "I've got a proposition to put to you, Cobb," he began then in a cheerful tone.

"Not for my benefit, I hope," growled the old warrior cynically.

Pat thought it time to bring him to order. "Don't trust anyone, do you? You've one less enemy, at any rate— according to your figuring," he said candidly. "Old Kip McKinley died this morning."

"What's that, Stevens? Kip's gone, you say—?" Russ broke in. Clearly the news daunted him. "That's one charge we're not saddled with, thanks to you!"

Not even Ben could pretend to ignore the announcement altogether. He looked at Pat slowly. "Well, now. . . . So you're layin' that at Stober's door, are yuh?"

Pat's nod was curt. "Stober killed McKinley—or ordered him shot. I'd swear to it. It could as easily have been your son, Cobb, instead of Kip," he reminded briefly. "Where is this going to end?"

Ben alerted. "Where?" he echoed gruffly. "That's if yuh know!"

Pat coolly outlined his plan to trap the War Ax owner into betraying open enmity. "That's something he's never done before—something the law is equipped to deal with," he pointed out. "Your troubles may not be over, but you'll know where you stand from now on. And so will Stober. He'll be forced to lay off the dirty work or keep his distance!"

Cobb let him finish. "Just exactly what is this fine scheme of yours?" he demanded with a stony expression.

Laying it on the line, Pat sought to emphasize the almost certain result of the pretended partnership with Colcord. At the end Ben burst out harshly, "You're askin' me to work with Crip Colcord! Why not the devil himself, and be done with it?" For him the only possible answer was self-evident. "Never in this world, Stevens! So now yuh know!"

"Dad, think this over a minute. You may be throwin' away your only chance to drag that wolf down," urged Russ. "If it's just a case of putting up a fence, that don't mean we owe Crip anything!"

"Who's payin' for it?" retorted Ben cagily.

"I will," Pat assured him. "This concerns us all, Cobb. I'm ready to carry my share of the load."

Ben thought it over and shook his head vigorously. "Nope. You're too willin', Stevens! If I can't buck Stober without Colcord's help, I'll go down tryin'. And that's final!"

Pat argued longer, but with no different result. Colcord had put a finger on the real flaw in his plan by citing Cobb's iron obstinacy. Wrongheadedness could go no further. Pat confessed as much to the Saw Buck owner when he rode into Colcord's ranch an hour after dark.

"I used enough hardheaded argument to convince a Chinaman," he averred as they talked it over in the kitchen. "Chain lightning will have to strike Ben Cobb before he sees the light!"

"So what *can* yuh do now?" Ezra asked.

"There's only one move left." Pat shrugged. "I may have to drag Jess Lawlor into this, much as I hate to— and talk to him like a Dutch uncle."

"Perhaps not, Pat," Penny spoke up in a low voice.

"That is, if you'll give me permission to try once more with Russ—"

They looked at her with half-awakened hope. "But that ain't the old man," reminded Colcord practically. "Will Russ be able to get anywheres with Ben either?"

She nodded readily. "I'm sure it will work," she said simply. "Can we afford not to try?"

Pat threw up his hands. "Russ will go along with it, I'm sure. If you can put it over where I failed, Penny, you're a dandy. And I won't be a bit surprised!"

There was more talk before they turned in. Not till the sun was an hour high the following morning, flashing over the sage with silver brightness and sharpening the crest of the Culebras, did the girl make ready to depart.

Pat suppressed the advice he had on the tip of his tongue as he watched her leave; but twenty minutes later the arrival of the Powder County sheriff thrust all thought of the girl from his mind for a time. Lawlor was investigating McKinley's death, and it suited Stevens to offer him a straightforward account of events, without embroidery of any kind.

Jess rode about the ranch, having his look and putting unhurried questions. It was long before he was done. Watching the sheriff jog away an hour after midday, no wiser than when he arrived, Pat awakened with a jar to the realization that Penny had not yet returned. He had expected her back long before this.

Colcord was even more on edge. "Hang it, boy! She's takin' time to ride to Denver and back," he complained.

"We'll shove over that way for a look around," Pat agreed. But as he saddled up he halted his preparations abruptly and gave a level glance across the range. "Here comes somebody now."

It was Penny. She was in no hurry, seeming to take ages to grow in size and draw near. Pat was waiting for her at the edge of the yard. He noted her look of pale firmness.

"Where were you?" he asked pointedly. "Did you ride over to War Ax, Penny—?"

Sliding down and letting him take the reins of the

horse, she nodded listlessly. "Yes, Pat. Why need I lie to you? I did go to see Mr. Stober."

Colcord came stumbling up as she ended. "What? What's that?" He was severe. "Don't yuh know that's the worst thing yuh could do, girl? . . . Givin' the whole game away," he fumed sourly, glaring at her. "Hanged if I didn't think yuh knowed better!"

Penny showed no resentment whatever, and little more spirit than before. "Father, he is not the fool you take him for—nor does he think us completely stupid," she summoned up the words patiently. "He has guessed that we are at least partially aware of his actions. Someone had to —reason with him." She broke off, her hands dropping. "I tried to."

"And did you get anywhere?" urged Pat gently.

"No, I—" She stumbled for adequate expression. "He answered me with—proposals that were completely preposterous. We couldn't get anywhere." Her look was tragic.

"Proposals, eh?" Old Crip bristled, caught despite himself. "What did he have to offer—not that it matters much!"

"I—It doesn't matter at all, Dad." For the first time she was hurried and evasive. "What he suggested was utterly impossible. I—prefer not to repeat it needlessly."

Colcord snorted his disdain. "So I suppose yuh never went near Antler or talked to young Cobb at all?" he snapped.

"Oh, yes. Russ brought me most of the way home," she assured. She looked at Pat beseechingly. "You're not angry with me? I told you I should almost certainly be able to persuade Russ—"

"No, Penny," replied Pat quietly. "And were you?"

Her nod had little of eagerness in it. "Yes. I waited until he talked with his father. Mr. Cobb has agreed to what you have planned to do."

Colcord showed great astonishment. "Yuh mean the old badger's agreed to look me in the eye and not fly straight off the handle—?"

"Yes, Dad. If you will undertake to do the same."

Caught between wind and water, old Crip could only grunt. "That's somethin' gained—if yuh persuaded Ben t' go even that far," he allowed moderately. "Danged if I thought he had it in him!"

[19]

"Get ready to travel, Colcord." Pat's composed tone was firm. "I don't like this any more than you do. But we'll have to ratify the deal and make some sort of arrangements."

The rugged old rancher groaned. "Yuh mean I got to go over there and take a chance of gettin' cuffed again?" But it was largely put on. Crip was willing enough. There was a suspicion of zest in the eagerness with which he made ready to start.

Sam saddled his horse for him. "Hanged if I don't think the old boy looks forward to lockin' horns with Cobb," he murmured disparagingly to Pat.

Stevens cracked a smile. "Not much different from Ez and you that way, is he?" he retorted amiably.

"Oh, go to grass," snapped Sam, waddling away with stiff dignity.

In excellent spirits now, Colcord was aware of their tiff, if not its cause. "Don't see why yuh put up with them crusty old codgers, Stevens," he commented, clambering astride.

"Don't you?"

"Well—" Sobering briefly, the Saw Buck owner gave him a shrewd look. "Rememberin' old Kip, maybe I do, at that. Kip didn't have a brain in his head, but there wasn't nothin' the matter with his heart."

Pat gave an understanding nod. "I'll tell Sam sometime what you think of him."

Crip snorted. "Yes, you will!" Grinning then, he felt that he and the other man understood each other.

Pat paused for a word with Ezra before they started away. "I needn't remind you and Sam to keep an eye on that girl while we're gone, Ez," he said.

The tall tracker glanced at him briefly. "We'll try."

Looking forward to the meeting in store for him, so different from the first visit to Antler, Colcord paid small heed to his surroundings as the two men crossed the range at a brisk pace. Pat made up for his lack of vigilance. But there was little to cause alarm as they covered the distance between and drew up on the Cobb ranch. Here Colcord took the time to glance about with attention.

"Poor old geezer ain't doin' too well, is he?" he remarked, noting the thinness of Ben's stock. "That could account for a part of his grouch the past few months."

Pat assented. "He's had to fight hard to hang onto what little he's got. And he's ready to go on fighting."

If Ben failed to show himself as they drew near, he was waiting in the house when they arrived. He stepped out warily at Pat's hail.

Colcord met his look without hostility. A change had occurred in him, subtle but unmistakable. Dismounting, he stumped forward. "Stevens gave me his rundown on our troubles, Cobb," he began mildly. "I think he's right. He says you're willin' to help trip Stober—and I figure he's hit on the right way to do that, too."

Ben nodded a curt assent, sniffing like a suspicious dog. "I'll go along with yuh just far enough to prove Stober's game and smash it," he allowed grudgingly.

"Slack off, Dad." Russ appeared from the direction of the corrals in time to catch the last sentence. "Pat and Crip are really trying to help us—and that don't call for any stuffy remarks."

"Oh, I don't know." Ben was cagey. "Colcord wouldn't be here if he wasn't helpin' himself, that's sure—"

"Good cripes!" Russ was vigorous and scornful. "You can't blame a man for that. We certainly can't pretend we're not hoping for the same result. But we can't do it alone. Let one hand wash the other—isn't that fair enough?"

Although he looked dubious, Cobb growled a muttered agreement. "I still don't get this partnership deal though," he insisted. "It means Colcord will be usin' Antler range to suit himself—but just let me try the same game!"

"There's where you're wrong." To Pat's surprise, Colcord broke in eagerly. "I'm not agreein' to no real partnership, no more than you would. But we'll give it out that we've made one, Cobb—and we got to make it look like one, at least enough to fool Stober!"

"At my expense, I suppose," grumbled Ben.

"No, no." Colcord was impatient. "Get Russ to shove that skinny Antler beef over on my range right off," he urged. "I won't begrudge the grass if it'll help square that range hoggin' deal yuh been squawkin' about."

Cobb looked briefly astonished. "Yuh mean that?" he demanded gruffly.

Even Russ was grinning at him. "What could be fairer than that, Dad?"

"But, now—" Frowning, Cobb evinced a slow change and softening of manner. But he was still not wholly convinced. "This range fence Russ is talkin' about. I don't just savvy the need for that!"

"It's the whole point," Pat put in quickly. "Let Stober tangle himself up in that wire. If he thinks you two have joined forces to block him off, he'll either be forced to let you—or toss his cards on the table fast. Didn't Russ or Penny explain?"

Ben nodded uncertainly. "I just don't aim to start nothin' I can't finish," he began.

"With me, yuh mean?" Colcord was stiffly good-humored. "Don't sweat none, Cobb. I ain't buyin' any more stock—and I don't want Antler. Once we get Stober licked, I'll have had enough of yuh both!"

"But this wire now," Ben said stubbornly. "It'll cost a few dollars."

"I'll supply the wire and the labor," Pat assured. "You

can trust Ezra and Sam, I expect. So if there's no serious argument against fencing off War Ax—"

"But, dang it, there is," exclaimed Cobb. "Stober'll kick—and kick hard!"

"Fine." Pat caught him up firmly. "That'll put us squarely in a position to kick back. There's six of us now —and we're not simply hired help. You're not afraid of the odds, Cobb?"

With this Ben was won over at last. There ensued further talk and planning, in which all worked together in apparent harmony. At the end Pat thought things were shaping up well.

"I'll get Sam and Ez started on that wire right off," he announced. "Ez can hire a couple of hands in Ganado and I'll send out a camp wagon. I don't want to appear in this, but I'll be handy. And remember," he warned them all, "if any War Ax punchers get curious, you don't know a thing. Let Stober guess. It won't take him long."

"I'm still working for him, Stevens—till I get my next pay," Russ put in soberly. "What if he asks me about this?"

Pat shrugged. "Ben hasn't told you what he and Colcord are up to, if anything. Offer to find out, if Stober insists. Will that do it?"

Russ thought it might. But it was plain that he foresaw complications. It was either that or quit, and he was afraid such a course would tip Stober off at once.

Returning to Saw Buck with Colcord, Stevens explained the situation to Ezra and Sam. All agog, the Bar ES partners were for immediate action. Pat dispatched Sam to Ganado for a load of wire, paying cash to forestall awkward questions. Ezra went with him to pick up a couple of hands, sending them to Saw Buck while he shoved on to Pat's Lazy Mare ranch to procure a camp wagon and supplies.

Things appeared meanwhile to have quieted down on the range, at least for a time. Penny and Colcord, the rancher fully recovered now, went about their usual work; Ben Cobb quietly drifted a portion of his herd over onto rich Saw Buck range, and still no unusual incident occurred.

By the afternoon of the second day the work of stringing up wire was commenced, and Pat rode out to see how it was getting along. Ezra was in charge.

"No trouble, I hope?" Pat queried.

The tall redhead shrugged. "Guess War Ax has been watchin' us," he allowed. "I spotted a puncher or two over that way. Nobody's come near yet."

Pat nodded. "Stober will be around soon," he predicted. "You know how to handle him. Did you plant the partnership yarn in town, as I suggested?" he pursued.

Ezra grunted. "Didn't have to. Just said I was hired to string wire—and when I was asked, I told where." He grinned wolfishly. "What else is there t' say?"

Pat nodded sagely. "It don't pay to overdo it," he agreed. "This will get to Stober fast, and then—bingo. Watch yourself, you and Sam."

Ezra did not seem to think the warning merited a reply. But two days later, on Monday morning, Sam rode hastily into Saw Buck, where Stevens was staying at intervals, on a saddleless horse, using the long straps of a wagon harness for reins.

"What's the trouble?" barked Pat, stepping into the yard behind Colcord.

"I was pullin' out of Ganado with a fresh load of wire, Stevens, and some hombre downed one of the horses!" Sam spat the words out savagely. "I made him scatter with my rifle, you bet. Get up your bronc, Stevens, and we'll go get us a horse killer!"

Pat waved this aside. "Snake another horse out of the pasture and haul that wire on where it belongs," he directed. "Colcord and I will ride out there with you, but I don't expect we'll find anything."

He and Crip rode out to the scene of the attack. While Sam worked the harness off the dead horse, hitched up and shoved on, they had their look around. They found the marksman's tracks, but lost them on rocky ground. Later the pair rode out to where the fence was going up. Sam had already told Ezra his troubles.

"No luck?" the one-eyed giant queried.

Pat shook his head. "How about you?"

"Stober was here, sure enough. He did some swearin', and rode off." Ez grinned, sobering as he glanced about. "Gil Smedley got shot at, cuttin' posts over here in the hills. No harm done." Smedley was one of the hands he had hired in Ganado. "What do yuh look for next, Stevens?"

Pat did not reply directly. "With a couple of miles of fence up, you'll be off of Cobb's range and onto Saw Buck by tomorrow. We can't watch it all—"

Ezra took his meaning. "Just be ready for anything, huh?"

"Shove along—and don't let anything surprise you," was the answer. "If this wire doesn't trigger an explosion before long, I'll miss my guess."

It did, that same night. As it happened, Russ Cobb was the first to discover what was afoot. The young fellow had had his worries during the last day or two. Against all expectation, Stober had said absolutely nothing to him, letting him fret it out. This looked ominous to Russ, and he had begun to fear for the success of Pat's plan. So much, in fact, that he took to riding the fence, in secret and at night, when he could not be accused of neglecting his work for War Ax.

That was how he came to be jogging along the lengthening line of posts and strung wire that had been stoutly erected under Ezra's direction, at an hour close onto midnight. Suddenly a sharp sound made him draw rein with a jerk. The late moon had waned, not rising till well on toward dawn; he could see little in the thick gloom. But a thundering rumble of stock could be heard some distance to the rear. Russ instantly realized the steers were running; he caught the muffled cries of riders.

"Blast it all! They're drivin' that stuff hard," he burst out sharply.

Turning back hastily, he barely made out that the racket came from the War Ax side of the line. Suddenly a trembling rolled up from the ground, augmented by the tormented bawling of cattle. The taut strands of the range fence twanged and sang, popping loudly as they snapped somewhere down the line, and then went slack, a post or two sagging drunkenly even at this distance. Thin dust assailed Cobb's nostrils.

He knew what it spelled. "Great Godfrey," he breathed. "They've rammed a hole in that fence, no matter how many broken legs or necks it cost!"

Instantly alert to his own position as an unexpected witness, he drew hastily back from the immediate area. Even now a shadowy rider drifted close, whirling his horse to peer in Cobb's direction. *"Who is that—you, Gyp?"* Russ made no response, fading into the gloom. An exclamation ripped out, followed instantly by the crash and flare of a gun.

There were yells and the pounding of horses' hoofs. There was more gunfire till an authoritative cry put an end to this. Rigidly holding his bronc to a soft trot, Cobb gradually drew apart. He was inwardly boiling, having recognized at once the harsh tones of more than one of Stober's renegade punchers.

There could be no serious question of what was happening here. Almost without thought Russ swung directly toward War Ax. Nearing the elaborate headquarters buildings twenty minutes later, he swung wide to enter the yard directly. Dismounting in a shadowy angle of the walls, he followed around to the alley leading to Stober's office.

At this late hour the office was dark, although never locked. Nor was anyone inside when he entered. Striding impatiently on through an inner door, Russ found himself in a maze of pitch-black hallways. He felt his way on determinedly. At length a dim glow of light showed from a distant door. Making for it, he pushed it noiselessly back and found himself confronted by Stober, seated at a table, the remains of a late meal at his elbow. A whisky bottle stood nearby.

"Deuce Dimock just rammed your herd through my father's new fence, Stober," cried Russ hotly. "I think you ordered it done, and I want to know the meaning of it!"

At sight of his visitor Stober's beady eyes flared up and then went cold. "And I want to know the meaning of that fence," he retorted harshly.

Russ stared with widening eyes. "Why, that's none of your affair," he whipped out flatly. "It doesn't touch War Ax anywhere—"

"Don't stall with me, boy," thundered Chuck.

Russ stilled. "Then I won't. . . . I'm not working for you anyway. I quit when that beef went through the wire," he announced dangerously. "You've showed your crooked hand, mister, trying to ruin Dad! I expect you had Kip McKinley put away too." The words rushed out so fast and furiously that Cobb seemed scarcely aware of what he was saying. "Furthermore, Penny swears Colcord must sell Saw Buck to War Ax and she must marry you if we're ever to expect peace." He broke off, breathing heavily. "That's blackmail, Stober—or worse!"

Stober grunted. "Is it? It might work, too," he replied stolidly, jabbing a thumb downward significantly and glancing past Cobb's shoulder.

Too fevered with rage to note the arrival of another man who appeared quietly in the door behind him, Russ whirled barely in time to see Dimock in the act of bringing a gun barrel down on his head. The heavy Stetson saved him the full force of the chopping blow, but lights flashed in his head and he felt himself falling. It seemed a long way down.

"Tie him up," Stober's growl reached him through a dreamy haze, "and toss him in there. Let 'em wonder where he went to for a while!"

He must have changed his mind in the end. The following afternoon found Gyp Carmer drifting warily across Saw Buck range, keeping to cover as much as he could. If he was looking for someone, he quit on sighting Penny Colcord riding about the range with several others.

The fence break had been discovered this morning, and all had worked hard to gather Stober's stock and shove it back through the gap. Ben Cobb had reported Russ's absence, and it was this which caused the girl her greatest concern. She asked Pat to refrain from retaliation until the puncher was found, and from the way she wandered without stopping, it was plain that she dreaded what she might find.

It was late when Carmer finally caught her isolated from the rest by a rocky butte, and rode forward boldly. Penny saw him coming. A fresh fear gripping her, she faced the sinister youth bravely.

"What are you doing on this range?" were her first uncompromising words.

Gyp wore a look of knowing confidence. "We got young Cobb," he announced, leering at her offensively. "Stober says yuh can buy him back though—"

Fury at his brazen effrontery blazed up in her. "Where is Russ now?" she demanded instantly.

His sole answer was to jerk a nod toward War Ax, watching her narrowly. The girl's eyes flashed. "Take me over there," she ordered curtly. Carmer obviously asked for nothing better, and she fell in behind him as he set off.

[20]

Gyp Carmer led the way into the War Ax yard, riding indolently. Penny was met promptly at the front entrance of the sprawling ranch house by Stober himself. It did not escape the girl that he had been waiting, and the knowledge did nothing to allay her uneasiness.

Stober stepped forward with an unaccustomed show of formality, holding her horse unnecessarily and smiling benignly up at her. "Get down, Penny," he invited.

His assured manner turned the smooth words into an order. Penny sat her saddle unmoving, gazing down at him with troubled eyes. "What have you done with Russ?" she demanded.

Stepping close, Stober reached up a beefy hand to

take her own, obliging her to step down. He turned her toward the door. "Come in, come in." He was falsely hearty.

"I hope you know what you're doin', Stober," called Gyp Carmer, standing by his horse. If it was a veiled warning, it fell on deaf ears. Stober turned to look at the puncher aloofly.

Pausing before the door, Penny had her own hasty glance about the range. It had been evening when the sinister Wax Ax kid had accosted her, and dark was now settling down. She did not like it. But if there was a chance of making her way to young Cobb she would not hesitate at the eleventh hour.

Tossing Carmer a curt order, Stober urged the girl on into the house. A glimpse of the comfortably furnished room to which she was conducted surprised but could not reassure her. She whirled on the big rancher.

"Russ isn't here! Where is he?"

Waving toward the chairs, Stober moved on to an inner door. "Deuce," he called into the darkness beyond. "Trot Cobb out here, will you?"

Standing tensely in the subdued light of a shaded lamp, Penny waited. She heard scuffling, a muttered word, and then the advancing sound of boots. Deuce Dimock appeared in the door. With a heave he hauled young Russ in after him. Cobb's legs were free, but his hands and arms were bound tightly behind his back. He had lost his hat, and wore a beaten, defiant look.

Stober returned his glare contemptuously. "This— squirt claims I tried to ruin Saw Buck," he announced with heavy sarcasm. "As if I had to try!" He looked across at Penny squarely, defying her to compare him with his captive. "It all depends on you, girl," he drove on with deadly calm, "whether I get any such idea in my head or not."

"Tell him to go to hell, Penny!" flashed Russ instantly, sucking in his breath. "He *did* try to ruin your dad; and now he's using pressure! I knew he was up to some such filthy trick!"

Stober deliberately let him finish, then gave a chilling

laugh. "Blow away, Cobb. That's scare stuff for kids," he scoffed. "As my father-in-law, Colcord needn't expect anything but help from me—and Penny knows it!" He walked over to stand close, smiling down at her. "Isn't that right?" he pressed inexorably.

Inward loathing seized her as she looked up into his unfeeling face. In his early fifties, Stober was blocky and bullnecked. Still in the full vigor of life, he obviously flattered himself that his masculine appeal for any smart girl must be strong, and that the difference between him and this twenty-year-old girl was negligible.

"I told you yesterday that I had no interest in your—offer," she said in a low, level tone.

"But you've thought it over," he urged with imperious self-confidence. "Come on, now. Don't be coy with me, Penny. I haven't time for tomfoolery—"

Penny stiffened bravely under this covert badgering. "Please release Russ," she ordered peremptorily. "And we'll go at once. I've no slightest wish to—be kittenish."

"You'll learn." He was guttural now, plainly approving her sturdy spirit. "Chances are you don't know what you're missing, girl. But I can teach you!"

There was a sharp tussle as he sought to put an arm around her. She struggled wildly, whirling away and striking at him defensively. "Cut it out, Stober!" cried Cobb, wrenching ineffectually at his bonds. His eyes were blazing. Even Deuce Dimock watched with an uneasy frown.

"Better take it a little easy if yuh want me around, boss," Deuce advised disgustedly. "I ain't above bustin' a fence or throwin' a little lead—but I don't go for rough stuff with women!"

Tense as she found her dilemma, Penny caught at the words. "Then you confess you're responsible for what happened last night?" she exclaimed sharply.

Deuce hesitated, glancing toward Stober, who coolly nodded. "I was there anyway," the puncher grunted.

"And I suppose you know something about the attack on Antler as well!"

"Maybe I do." Deuce was growing surly. "But that ain't neither here nor there, as I see it—"

Glaring at Stober, however, Penny read in his triumphant bearing his reason for letting her know the worst. Chuck's cold nod was the clincher. "You see how easy it would be to avoid such—unfortunate occurrences," he suggested boldly.

She stared at him, dread in her heart. "I can—believe almost anything of you now," she whispered.

"I don't mind. Why, shucks! D'you want a real man, Penny? Or a milksop like Cobb here? Come on, girlie—" Once more he tried masterfully to encircle her in his arms.

Again she fought fiercely, striking ineffectually at his face. Stober's laugh was grating. There was in him the driving passion to subdue her resistance under Russ Cobb's jealous eyes. Possessing twice her size and weight, in a matter of seconds his brute strength had her helpless, bent backward but still violently avoiding his bristly face.

"Blast it, Stober! *I said quit!*"

It was Dimock who unleashed this violent blast. Cobb was likewise adding vehemently to the uproar. Vaguely enjoying all this, aware that he was bending more than one person to his ruthless will, Stober was abruptly alarmed by the sudden consciousness of silence. For a second he failed to gather what it was that had interrupted his self-confidence. He paused, his head coming up. Then he saw the dim figure of a silent newcomer standing in the front door and almost filling it.

Stober straightened slowly, releasing Penny with a self-conscious laugh. He had recognized Pat Stevens. Fully aware that he was caught far over the line on forbidden ground, he sought to worm out of it with his usual oily suavity.

"So there yuh are, Stevens! Caught us sparkin', did yuh?" It must have taken tremendous effort to speak this lightly.

Stevens did not reply directly. "Stand away from him, Penny." He was dangerously calm.

Stober saw the meaning of his position in Pat's stony face. "No you don't!" he rasped, making a grab at the girl's wrist before she could move. "Stay where you are, girl—" A scuff of boots and the voices of Sam and Ezra coming from the door at that moment further alarmed him.

Flashing a look around, Stober saw that Deuce Dimock had silently faded from the scene. Chuck had thrown the hard-boiled puncher's tough loyalty away by persisting in his blind foolishness with this girl. Still he had a trick or two left.

"Dimock, Carmer, Grady!" he roared toward the inner door, turning his head that way. "Nail these birds! The boys'll get 'em from behind!" As he hurled the order, hoping to turn Pat's hard attention from himself, his right hand streaked to his Colt.

It came up crashing. He had reckoned without Penny's fighting spirit, however. Violently jostling his arm, she succeeded in deflecting that deadly point-blank aim. The slug slapped harmlessly into the wall.

Even as Stevens leaped forward the burly War Ax owner dodged aside, thrusting Penny out of his way. With a stamp of boots, just as Ezra and Sam appeared belatedly in the door, Stober slammed heavily into Russ Cobb, knocking him reeling, then dived into the rear part of the house.

"Run the wolf down, boys!" Setting the example, Pat sprang after the fugitive while Penny rushed to Russ Cobb and started to work feverishly at his bonds. The grizzled partners had followed Stevens, and could be heard clattering in hot pursuit through the maze of the big house.

"Russ, I was never so afraid for us both!" the girl panted.

"You didn't show it." Cobb's gruffness held undisguised admiration. "Hurry it up, Penny! He can't get away now—"

Ezra burst back into the room as he was shaking off the last of his bonds.

"You lost him, Ez?"

"He got outside," the big man tossed back. "Come on, boy! We got to cut him off from them horses!"

They rushed out. It was dark now, but Ezra led the way around the house. In the direction of the corrals Mexicans could be heard calling on their saints as they scattered. Yells rang out. Pat and Sam had apparently reached the open by another way, and were closing up on Stober.

"There he goes!" It was Sloan. "Swing around wide— cut him off over there!"

Stober was making a determined attempt to reach a fast horse. Roaring authoritatively once for support, without visible result, he realized that his confederates had prudently decamped, and thereafter he remained silent. Dodging about the corrals, ducking as running feet pounded close, he worked as fast as he could. Even the nervous horses seemed trying to balk him. Savagely mastering one, indifferent to the lack of a saddle, he swarmed astride.

Stevens caught the driving splatter of hoofbeats. "Watch it! He's on a bronc!" He fired once fruitlessly, turned, then raced for his own mount.

The others came pelting from various directions. Russ found his bronc where it still stood in the shadows. He swept out into the thickening gloom.

"This way!"

It was Pat who guided them. He turned Stober back from his desperate attempt to reach open range. All scattered out, sternly seeking the elusive quarry in muffling blackness. Hoofs pounded sharply, and sudden cries broke out.

"Turn him back! Turn him back!" Ez roared as a ghostly shadow shot past him, thrashing the brush.

Before they were able to corner him, the dodging fugitive won to the open. Still they could hear Stober careering wildly on. "Swing him east," called Pat sharply. Like punchers crowding a stubborn steer, they drove Stober on but could not pin him down. In a matter of minutes they were nearing the edge of War Ax range.

"Watch for that drift fence," sang out Russ warningly. "It runs along here somewhere—"

"Why do yuh suppose we're drivin' that slick-ear this way?" retorted Sam harshly. "It'll turn him back, Cobb —and then's when we'll bag him!"

Whether Stober sensed his perilous position could not be determined. He dodged and evaded without being able to break back. Once Cobb thought the man must be flitting close, and he strained his sight to pierce the gloom. Then came a twanging, wiry clash, somewhere close ahead, followed by the agonized scream of a horse and a man's frenzied cursing.

"He's hit it," Pat rang out. "Watch which way he turns—"

Russ was already closing in, driven by savage rage. Peering hard, he made out a bulky form struggling on the ground. Stober's horse! The animal had been knocked off its feet, fearfully slashed by the wire barbs. It had thrown its rider sprawling. The horse tried to struggle up, fighting Stober's iron grip on the reins at the same time.

"*Get up.* On your hocks, you devil!"

"Hold it, Stober—right where you are!" flashed Cobb, leaping down and dashing in. Stober saw him coming. His six-gun flashed aimlessly, stabbing the dark with an orange flame. Russ smashed into him and the gun went flying.

Wrenching away, Stober turned and fled. Knocked to his knees, Russ sprang up and leaped after. Racing in Stober's wake, he overhauled him swiftly and was in the act of stretching out a grasping hand, when the man went headlong with a yell and a *twang-g-g!* of wire. In the dark Stober had sprinted squarely into the scattered tangle of loose strands left there the night before by the charging War Ax herd.

"Ow-w-w! Get me up—!" bawled the luckless rancher. Barely managing to stop himself, and hastily catching at Stober's waving arm, Russ heaved him up. Half-erect, Chuck treacherously unleashed a stunning blow at the young fellow, just as Stevens and the others came running.

Whirling then, Stober tried once more to spring away, only to trip afresh and go down heavily, the entangling wires gripping him cruelly. This time he was too severely punished to attempt further protest as Sloan lit a brush torch, and the others ungently disengaged him from the looping wires and hauled him to his feet.

Ez peered at him in the flickering light. "Humpf! Yuh look like a case of malignant measles, Stober," he growled. "Sort of set the trap for yourself, yuh might say——"

Gashed and bloody, Stober sought to outstare them. He couldn't make it, his chin sinking on his heaving chest. Meanwhile the flare of the torch had been seen. Old Colcord and Ben Cobb came riding up, their fighting jaws outthrust.

"Who is that . . . ? *Stober?* Then yuh ain't found Russ yet!" Cobb jerked out harshly.

"Here I am, Dad. And we've got Stober cold." Russ spoke up sturdily despite his own stinging scratches. "What will we do with him, Stevens?"

"We'll hold him while somebody goes for Sheriff Lawlor," Pat said. "But I expect to go back there and pick up Penny first——"

"I'm here, Pat." The girl spoke from the shadows. "Somehow, I—had to follow."

"Well, now," old Ben said severely. "What are yuh doin' over here at this hour, girl? What happened—and how come Stober wound up tangled in that wire?"

Russ told the story in rushing words. Colcord was fuming with rage before the end. "And I was arguin' for that rattler? . . . Why bother Lawlor?" he snarled. "There's a handy cottonwood over here a ways——"

The words alerted Stober as no recriminations could do. Fear tore his darting eyes wide. But for once Ben Cobb was deeply curious, peering at him keenly.

"What about it, mister? Will yuh buy a few years in the pen by admittin' you set us at each other—ordered old McKinley knocked off—ripped out our fence, and a few other small matters?"

Abjectly defeated by pain and hopelessness, Stober hurriedly nodded. "I'll—talk," he promised huskily.

"What about that wolf pack you've had running this range, Stober?" Pat struck in firmly. *"Was* it by your order, they tried to rob Colcord, shot up Antler, and set on Kip McKinley when he was without help?"

Chuck could only hang his head in mute confession. "I'll testify to it all, Stevens. . . . But you'll never nail those boys. They've pulled out like rats from a burnin' barn!"

"If they keep goin' fast enough and far enough, that won't matter," averred Sam hardily.

"Wait a minute." Ben Cobb was stern. "Are yuh fully admittin' yuh turned Pack Traver loose on me and the boy so yuh could grab T Square when it was all over, Stober?"

"Yes, yes—I can explain everything!" The big man was pleading now. "Hurry up and get me to a doctor!"

Ben ignored his discomfort. "Well—all right. I can spare a hangin' for the sake of havin' the truth come out all around," he declared firmly. "Does that go for you too, Colcord?"

"Ain't so sure." Crip pretended great reluctance, gazing toward the coiled rope on his saddle. "If Stober pays for his scurvy works, I suppose it'll have t' do."

"Here's one partnership anyway, that paid off," commented Sam sagely, on a rising note of good humor. "You two old duffers better like it too," he told Cobb and the Saw Buck owner impudently. "Because from here it looks like it's goin' to be permanent—"

"What *are* yuh drivin' at, Sloan?" Old Colcord bristled, his lips quivering.

It was Ezra who briefly explained, thumbing significantly toward Penny and young Russ, standing close together on the edge of the shadows and obviously in full accord with each other regardless of the differences of their parents.

"There's your answer," Ez murmured, turning his back politely, a twinkle in his single eye. "Looks to me like them two have declared peace, Colcord. That'll go for both of yuh, o' course. And if yuh ain't goin' to like takin' orders from grandchildren, yuh better make up

your minds to become silent partners—and in short order, at that!"

The accuracy of Sam's crusty prediction was pointed
up by the crooked smiles that broke simultaneously on
the mouths of both elderly ranchers.